When everything seems a
always found escaping int
book invariably makes n

For a few hours, you can ~~ transported to
another era, drawn into a beautiful romance or
whisked away to an exotic destination. Bliss!
Fiction is the perfect way to soothe the soul, so
why not take time out to relax and unwind with
these great short stories, hand-picked from the
archives of My Weekly magazine?
Penned by your favourite bestselling authors,
including Adele Parks, B.A. Paris, Milly Johnson
and Claudia Carroll, we've come up with an
extra-special selection of stories that are sure to
provide the perfect little escape.
Romance, laughter, rekindled passions, touching
tales of new beginnings – you'll find it all!
Now, put your phone to one side, pour some tea
(or a glass of wine), find a cosy spot to curl
up in and… relax!

Susan Watson,
Commissioning
Fiction Editor,
My Weekly magazine

© DC Thomson & Co Ltd, 2020
Published in Great Britain by D C Thomson & Co. Ltd.,
185 Fleet Street, London EC4A 2HS
www.dcthomson.co.uk

ABBIE GREAVES

HELEN LEDERER

RACHEL HORE

VIVIEN BROWN

ROSANNA LEY

JANE CORRY

LORNA COOK

B.A. PARIS

EMMA CURTIS

CATHY BRAMLEY

MILLY JOHNSON

SARAH MORGAN

ADELE PARKS

ISABELLE BROOM

ANNIE MURRAY

PHOEBE MORGAN

JO THOMAS

CLAUDIA CARROLL

CONTENTS

ADELE PARKS

First
Impressions

Sarah was missing the thrill of romance, but where could she find the right man for her?

S arah sank back into her couch, balancing her tea and biscuits. She took a moment to admire the tidy environment she'd re-established.

She loved the children coming home from university for the weekend. She liked to hear their news, and to see them eat properly. Sarah admitted that at nineteen and twenty-one years old, her offspring were on paper adults, but they still seemed very young to her.

Life was often tough, stressful and expensive, harder than when she and Liam started out; the children often seemed as vulnerable as they were on their first day of school.

She encouraged them to visit. She didn't mind the extra work.

That said, they were incredibly messy. White towels became bruised with smudges of mascara, jars and bottles repelled their lids, bins spat out litter and tables were tattooed with coffee cup rings.

Sarah's cleaner came every Wednesday and had been doing so for years. Sarah couldn't live in this mess until Wednesday, so she tidied up herself. Besides, Maggie was not an especially effective cleaner; anything beyond light dusting was a stretch.

Still, Sarah wouldn't dream of firing Maggie after many years of devotion (as Liam had done to Sarah). Maggie needed the extra money – and quite honestly, Sarah liked the company.

Sarah remembered thinking she was entitled to a cleaner, it was a social status thing. There were certain things a woman like her was supposed to have – a detached property, a cleaner, a window cleaner, a husband in the city.

She hadn't been able to hold on to her husband, but she was determined to cling on to the rest.

Their divorce had been relatively amicable. Liam moved to Hong Kong with his younger, prettier, blonder (sillier!) PA. Sarah got the family home and enough cash. Guilt motivated him to find his way to a squabble-free divorce.

Sarah didn't miss Liam any more; he was absent long before they had divorced.

She sipped her tea and surveyed the now dust-free surfaces, the neatly stacked magazines and the polished floorboards with the same pleasure as other women ogled George Clooney.

A tap at the front door disturbed her.

"Afternoon, Sarah."

Sarah would have preferred it if Michael, the window cleaner, called her Mrs Jackson; Sarah seemed too familiar. She tried to call him Mr Simmons (the name on his van); he'd make a joke about his dad being retired and insisted she call him Mike; they compromised with Michael.

"Can you refill my bucket, please?" Michael asked with a polite smile. He always asked for fresh water now, which Sarah loved. It was an unequivocal joy to her when the sunlight bounced through her streak-free windows. "Have you been cleaning?" he asked, craning his neck into the spotless hallway. "Looks like I could eat my dinner off your floors!"

Michael was always cheerful and made pleasant small talk. On cold, blowy days he commented how fresh everything was; on a hot day he said it was lovely weather to be outside.

Liam had always been dour; he didn't "do" chat. Not that it was ➔

fair to compare. Mike was a window cleaner and therefore carefree and with little responsibility, while Liam had an important job with a great deal of stress. He never noticed Sarah's polished surfaces.

"Would you like a cold drink? I've some delicious home-made lemonade. It wasn't made in this home. Farm shop purchase. The children visited, and we went for a bracing country walk."

Michael followed her.

"How are the kids? Working hard?"

"Fine, I think. The only thing they worry about is me. This month Amanda suggested I download a dating app. Last month she suggested a night class." Sarah rolled her eyes. "She thinks I'm short on company."

"Are you?"

"Not at all."

Michael had been cleaning Sarah's windows for five years. For four of them they'd barely spoken. Sometimes she'd sit inside a room while he cleaned the windows outside. She wouldn't acknowledge him; instead she'd bury her nose in her novel.

> She was surprised to discover that he was extremely easy to talk to

Sarah didn't mean to be rude; she just didn't know what to say to him. What could they have in common?

Then, about a year ago, Michael asked for some clean water and she obliged.

Naturally, they shared a few words. Now they had a cup of tea or juice together almost every week.

Sarah was surprised to discover she found Michael very easy to talk to. He knew all about the trials of her children's exams, he understood her anxiety as to whether she ought to move her fiercely independent father into an assisted living flat. How far must a good daughter go? He knew a lot about her life.

She knew nothing of his. He wore a wedding ring, so she thought any enquiry she might make would seem inappropriate. She also thought it would be inappropriate to admit that yes, sometimes she was short of a certain type of company.

She nervously searched around for a new topic of conversation. Suddenly Michael seemed very big and very male, standing in her neat and gleaming kitchen.

Michael's eyes flicked around the room and then settled – with some relief – on Sarah's novel.

"What are you reading?"

"It's the book group's choice."

"Any good?"

Michael picked up the book and started to read the blurb on the back cover. Irrationally, Sarah felt embarrassed. She wasn't sure whether it was the sort of book a window cleaner would enjoy. It was very deep and complex. It was a novel split into two parts; half set in nineteenth-century India, the other part twenty years in the future.

"I'm enjoying it."

"Why?"

Sarah always had a book on the go, sometimes two. She loved diving into stories and living other people's lives for a short time. She enjoyed being challenged, exploring the world and growing her vocabulary, all from the comfort of her front room. But when anyone ever asked her about why she enjoyed reading she found it impossible to articulate.

"Oh, it's erm, unexpected," she mumbled. "Fancy a biscuit?'

I think he sounds interesting," said Cath, with a cheeky, wink-wink grin that Sarah knew and dreaded.

"Who sounds interesting?" asked Liz.

"Sarah's window cleaner."

"Oughtn't we to talk about the book?" asked Sarah.

It frustrated her that every month the book group followed the same chaotic course. Wine would be poured, nibbles handed round, chatter and gossip would flow. The book would be forgotten. ➤

9

"We can't start yet – not everyone's here," said Julie. "We're expecting a new member."

The worst thing about the gossip, as far as Sarah was concerned, was that the others tended to focus on her. They all had partners and were either blissfully happy or horribly miserable; and it seemed that neither state was as fascinating as her single status. Since Liam left her, it appeared that the book group's raison d'être was to find Sarah a new man.

Sarah was reluctant. It was difficult to imagine meeting anyone new. When pressed as to what she wanted in a man, she would say that she wanted someone steady, financially secure, diligent.

"Dull, you mean," objected Cath the first time she heard the prosaic list.

"I mean someone like Liam."

"But Liam had an affair and left you."

Cath had resisted adding that Liam was dull.

"Like Liam but without the affair," admitted Sarah.

"Well, I think you should try something – someone – totally different," insisted Cath.

Now Cath was fascinated by Sarah's window cleaner; the thought terrified Sarah. Cath was a force to be reckoned with when she latched on to an idea. Sarah blushed at the thought of dating her window cleaner. She had to nip the idea in the bud instantly.

"He's not my type," she protested.

"You don't have a type, there's only ever been Liam," said Liz.

"Window cleaners earn pretty good money nowadays, you know," added Julie.

Sarah blushed.

"It's not the money. I don't need money. It's –" She didn't know how to phrase it without sounding snobby. "I don't think we'll have that much to talk about."

"You said you find him easy to talk to."

Cath shrieked with laughter again and made a joke about the importance of finding a man who is good with his hands. The token male group member, Ian, wriggled uncomfortably on his chair.

The doorbell rang, saving Sarah.

"Can I introduce Mike Simmons?" said Julie with a beam.

For a nano-second Sarah didn't recognise Michael. She knew his face as well as the back of her hand, but seeing him out of context and in smarter clothes startled her.

He startled all the other female group members too. They sat with backs straight and chests out, grinning and wide-eyed.

"Take a seat next to Sarah," said Cath, pointing to the free chair. Sarah smiled at Michael but before they had chance to say they knew one another, Ian seized the moment to talk about the book.

"I don't suppose you've had chance to read it yet, have you, Mike?"

"I just picked it up this week but managed to finish it this morning."

"Good going. It's chunky, isn't it?"

"Yes – but fascinating."

"What did you like about it, Mike?" Cath enquired.

"I was transported. The descriptions were lyrical. The characters were so complex and believable, even though their dilemmas were very removed from my own experience."

Sarah froze. She thought she might be ill on Julie's hall carpet

Sarah couldn't agree more. She nodded enthusiastically but somehow couldn't find her tongue.

For the rest of the evening Sarah listened as Michael enthused about books. He was familiar with many classics and most of the recent prize winners. He'd read lots of the books Sarah had bought but had never got around to. He had an opinion on them all.

Sarah was enthralled by each well-observed point he made and mesmerised by his perception and confidence. How had she known him for five years and not known him at all? After all, he knew all about her.

He must think her so snobby and prejudiced, she thought with dismay. Why had she let her sensibility prevent her from getting to ➔

know him better? Shivers of terror ran up her spine – she had to ensure the others did not resume the conversation about her window cleaner.

She waited for a pause and an appropriate moment to mention her relationship with Michael. None came.

Sarah remained tense all evening. She struggled to find the arm of her coat. Over and over she jabbed at her sleeve but couldn't twist in the correct way.

Michael helped her.

"Thanks." A blush flared up on her neck and crept up to the roots of her hair.

"You were very quiet this evening. I thought you liked the book."

"I did. It's just that –"

"She's shy." Cath appeared at their side. She lived five minutes' walk from Julie's and so had seen off almost a bottle of wine. Thus fortified, she asked, "Are you married?"

"Widowed, actually."

"Oh," said Sarah. "Sorry."

"Nine years ago now. Look, maybe we could go for a coffee and you can tell me your thoughts on the book without a crowd," said Michael to Sarah.

"Don't waste your time, Mike. You're not her type," grinned Cath. Sarah froze.

"She has a type?" asked Michael, with a curious and friendly grin. Sarah thought she might be ill on Julie's hall carpet.

"Yes – she's after a bit of rough. She fancies her window cleaner. You, sir, are far too educated," joked Cath.

"That's interesting," said Michael. Sarah wouldn't meet his eye, but she could feel his boring into her. "Do you think it's fair to have such preconceptions? Couldn't you give me a chance?"

Sarah forced herself to look up.

"You're right. There's nothing worse than pre-conceptions. I'd love a coffee." Ⓜ️

JO THOMAS

Ice-Cream And Future Dreams

So many flavours – how can Nancy ever make her choice?

Nancy stood and stared, rooted to the spot, gripped by indecision. A cacophony of colours swirled in front of her eyes. She reached out a hand to the clear glass, resting her fingertips there, finding comfort in its coolness.

She didn't think she'd ever seen that many colours before. Soft folds of pink, swirls of deep cerise, mounds of bright green, balls of bright blue and layers of deep, dark brown. A whole rainbow laid out like a glorious landscape. Mounds upon mounds, like a mountain range.

She felt much cooler now – cool enough, in fact, to slip her sweatshirt on – and her head had stopped thumping. Away from the early morning August heat, from the villa and "the wait", suddenly she felt in an oasis of calm. The outside world was exactly that, out there. The worries of the day, the months of hard work, were all a world away in here.

She looked around at the small, empty ice-cream parlour, with towers of biscuit cones on top of the gleaming glass freezer, bottles ➤

ILLUSTRATION: ISTOCKPHOTO, MANDY DIXON

13

of sauces along the high counter, jars of sprinkles on the shelves behind, reflected in the mirrors there, making the tiny shop look bigger. And in front of her, the freezer full of every kind of ice-cream you could imagine.

She ran her finger along the glass, reading the Italian for each of the flavours and then, as there seemed to be no one around, saying them out loud, liking the way the words felt as they rolled off her tongue.

She started with, "Gelato!" Ice-cream! She smiled. It had been a lovely week at the villa she and her friends had rented after all the hard work leading up to their exams. An end-of-exams celebration and eighteenth birthday present all in one.

"Cioccolato," she said, enjoying the feel of the sound.

She was excited to spend time with her friends again. There had been no time before their A-levels. Revision had taken up all her spare time, keeping up with her carefully planned timetable.

He handed her a small pot. "Try this one, tell me what you taste"

Everyone had high hopes for Nancy. Her mother was already telling people the college she would be going to and how she planned to be a doctor – just like her and her father.

It was how it had always been; it was just expected that that was what she'd do, and so she had. She'd made the right A-level choices, applied to universities and – depending on her exam results later that morning – she'd be on track to follow exactly in their footsteps.

"Fragola," she said, and repeated it more slowly because she liked the way it sounded. "Fra…go…la."

Her parents were going to the school to pick up her results, insisting she should relax in the sun after all her hard work. She felt far from relaxed when she'd woken early that morning. But here, in the cool of the ice-cream parlour, relaxed was exactly how she felt.

"Fragola, cioccolato," she repeated, smiling to herself. "Ciocc…"

"May I help you?"

Nancy jumped and stopped mid-flow. A dark-haired young man appeared from behind a fly curtain, which tinkled like little bells as it fell back into place.

"Sorry, I was just attending to a new batch of ice-cream." He pointed in the direction of the back room. "Now, what can I get you?"

He smiled widely and she stared at him, in awe of his perfect English.

"Um, I don't know," said Nancy, still unable to make up her mind as she looked at the brilliant display of ice-cream mounds behind the cool glass.

She felt torn between looking at the beautiful array and the very good-looking young man smiling at her, his eyes the same colour as the cioccolato ice-cream.

"I usually just go for caramel," she confessed. It had been her favourite since she was a girl.

"What you need to do is try a little of everything before you decide," he said enthusiastically. "All the ice-creams are made here in Sicily, in our town of Città d'Oro, from the cows that live here side by side with the lemon trees."

Nancy found herself catching her breath and blushing at his passion, a fire starting to burn within her own stomach. She looked down at the row of ice-creams again, trying to distract herself from his beautiful eyes and bright smile.

"This ice-cream comes from the heart of our island," he said, and once again Nancy blushed and wished she felt that same kind of passion about her life and her chosen career.

Or was it even her chosen career? She couldn't remember choosing to be a doctor – it's just what it was always assumed that she would go on to be.

Her other friends in the villa had so much more passion for the courses they wanted to be accepted for and where they hoped life would take them. Mair played saxophone and wanted to study music, Alice wanted to be an architect and was soaking up the Sicilian stonework made from the lava of Mount Etna. And Tia wanted to ➤

study law, as if her life depended on it; she wanted to fight the injustices in the world.

Nancy, she realised, simply didn't want to let her parents down.

"Here." The young man was handing her a small pot, with a spoon in it. "Try this one and tell me what you taste."

His gaze made her insides flutter as their fingertips touched. A small trickle of ice-cream ran down the side of the pot. She licked it away, smiling at him as he watched her.

She put the spoon in her mouth, loving the coolness, letting it sit there until it melted and finally swallowing, enjoying every bit of its creamy, soft flavour.

"I don't know. It's beautiful, but it doesn't taste of anything in particular," she said. "Just, well, like ice-cream should... creamy!"

"That's our plain ice-cream, just the taste of milk and sunshine." He smiled, as warmly as the Sicilian sun. Then he lined up three more little pots for her to try.

"Strawberry." She smiled.

"Fragola," he corrected her and they both laughed.

"Coffee. No – is it almond?" She was unsure.

"Biscotti," he corrected. "The little biscuits we have with coffee here."

She tried chocolate and pistachio, and then one more.

"Wow!" She laughed. "Popping candy!"

He laughed too, making her laugh even more, something she hadn't done for months now.

"Surprise! Life is full of surprises once you start to taste it! There are lots of colours and flavours out there. Maybe you should take time to try them all!"

He grinned and something in Nancy shifted. He was right. There were a lot of flavours out there. Ones she'd never tried.

"Now, which ones would you like?" He held up a shiny silver bowl. Her lips were still sweet from the tastings.

"There you are!"

Nancy turned to see her best friend, Mair, standing behind her.

"How did you know where to find me?" Nancy asked, bewildered.

She had texted her friend only to say that she was going for a walk to clear her head.

"Because you always turn to ice-cream." Mair smiled.

"True," said Nancy. "When all else fails, there is always ice-cream."

The young man behind the counter filled the bowl with three big scoops and two spoons sticking out of it.

"This is…" Nancy hesitated and Mair looked between the pair of them.

"Nico," he said politely. "Would you care to join us, on the terrace?"

He pointed to the stone steps leading down to a covered terrace with pots of geraniums, overlooking a lemon grove.

"I was just introducing…"

"Nancy," Nancy finished for him.

"Nancy to our ice-cream flavours."

Mair hesitated then raised a hand, spotting the two spoons.

Just one bowl of ice-cream before discovering what her future held

"No. It looks delicious, but I'll leave you two to it. I just came to tell you I got my grades! Mum just messaged. I'm going to music college!" She beamed.

"Whoop!" Nancy hugged her friend tightly, so pleased she'd found where she wanted to be in life and felt a pang of envy.

Would she feel the same if she got her grades today? Or would she just imagine how pleased her parents would feel?

"Right, I'm off back!" said Mair. "Let me know when you have your results!"

"Will do!" said Nancy and in that instant she felt her phone vibrate in her pocket. She didn't want to answer straight away. Instead she waved Mair off and followed Nico.

"I'll listen out for the bell over the door. Fortunately, it seems too early for most people to have ice-cream."

It was never too early for Nancy.

He led her down the worn stone steps, out onto the terrace, ➔

looking over the lemon groves to the sparkling sea beyond.

Nancy caught her breath and sighed. It was heaven. She could smell the lemon blossom in the air, mixed with the fresh sea breeze and wondered if that could be an ice-cream flavour.

"Please, sit." Nico smiled again seeing her reaction to the little walled terrace, watching her face taking it all in.

"You seemed unable to decide, so I chose for you," he said softly, putting the bowl between them.

Nancy sat, knowing she should check her messages. But it could wait – just until she'd eaten the ice-cream. Just one bowl of ice-cream before discovering what her future held.

Either way, she realised, she was going to be disappointed. Disappointed if she didn't get the grades after all her hard work – and disappointed if she did, because she simply didn't feel as Mair did about the plans for her life, all mapped out for her.

Their spoons clashed and a fizz of excitement bubbled in Nancy

"So, we have the popping candy, the cherry... and this one is my favourite," he said, lifting a spoon for Nancy to try.

She took the mouthful.

Oh, my word! Her eyes widened, looking at Nico.

"That is amazing!" she said. "That's... the taste of here!" She gazed at the citrus trees that surrounded them.

He nodded. "Limone, plain and simple. The taste of Sicily."

"I love it," she said and dipped her spoon in for more, as did Nico.

"Like I say, you have to try a lot of flavours to find the right one for you. But I'm glad you like the same as me." He smiled and Nancy felt her insides melt, like the ice-cream on her tongue.

"So, your friend is off to college?" he asked. "And you?"

Nancy sighed, pulling out her phone and putting it face down on the table.

"I thought I had life mapped out... but my plans might have changed. I'm about to find out," she said as she went in for the last scoop of ice-cream, at the same time as Nico. Their spoons clashed and another fizz of excitement bubbled up in Nancy as they both laughed and he insisted she have the last mouthful as she'd finally found the one she loved.

"You have to find the one that makes your heart sing."

Back at the villa, the prosecco was ready to be popped. "Hey! Here she is! What's the news?" Her friends looked at her eagerly.

"I got the grades!" Nancy said brightly and they cheered, but stopped as they went to hug her and she held up a hand.

"But…" She took a deep breath. "I've decided to have a gap year!" They looked at her, shocked.

"I don't know if being a doctor is what I want; if it's my choice or just what everyone expects me to do. I'm going to have a year out. Travel a bit. See more of this island. Taste more ice-cream! I'm even going to have a go at making some with Nico this evening… creating my own flavour."

Suddenly she smiled and her friends did too, knowing that she'd made exactly the right choice.

"By the way, what flavour ice-cream did you go for in the end?" Mair asked.

"All of them. The only way to find out what you really love is to try a little of everything. That's what I'm going to do, try a little of everything to find something I love!" she said, thinking of Nico.

With that, they popped the prosecco and toasted each other's future happiness… and ice-cream.

Because whatever happens in life, there is always ice-cream. 🔵

B.A. PARIS

Keeping Secrets

Wedding dress shopping is fraught at the best of times – let alone when there's bad news to tell

Helen had been looking forward to today for months. But now, when she saw Jenny waving to her from the other side of the road, all she felt was dread.

How do you tell your best friend, on the day that you're going to help her choose a wedding dress, that her husband-to-be is having an affair?

She watched Jenny dash across the road. She looked so happy, so excited.

Helen hated that she was going to break her heart but she couldn't let Jenny marry a man who was cheating on her.

She wished she hadn't seen Carl with the woman who was young enough to be his daughter. But she had – not once, but twice.

"Thank you for taking a day off work," Jenny said, giving Helen a hug. "There's nobody I'd rather have by my side today. The first appointment is at ten, so we'd better hurry."

Helen couldn't let Jenny try on wedding dresses when the wedding might never take place.

"Could we go and have a coffee first, do you think?" she asked, her heart heavy with dread.

Jenny checked her phone.

"Sorry, it's already five to. I've got so much to tell you but we'll have to talk over lunch." She linked her arm through Helen's. "So, how are you?"

"I'm good," Helen lied. "How's Carl?"

"He's fine, better than he's ever been," Jenny said happily.

I bet he is, Helen thought resentfully. *How could he? How could he cheat on someone as lovely as Jenny?*

She'd been at Waterloo, heading to the bookshop to buy something to read on the train home, when she'd seen Carl standing outside Foyles. She was just about to wave to him, glad to have someone to travel with, when a young woman came running up and threw herself into his arms.

It wasn't the sort of hug that you might give a friend; it was a long, tight, never-want-to-let-you-go hug that went on for so long Helen had felt embarrassed just watching.

She'd turned away, trying to tell herself that she was mistaken, that it wasn't what she thought. But when she looked back, Carl and the woman – pretty, blonde, petite – had been staring into each other's eyes.

"Here it is," Jenny said, coming to a stop outside the bridal boutique. "I've looked at their website and they have some lovely dresses. And if I don't find one here, we have another appointment this afternoon."

Jenny – pretty, but not blonde or petite – tried on eight dresses and looked lovely in all of them.

"But which do you like best?" she asked Helen anxiously. "They're all very different so there must be one that suits me more than the others."

"The second one you tried on," she told Jenny. "You looked absolutely stunning."

She still didn't know if the tears that had sprung to her eyes were because of the dress or because she knew that Jenny might never get to wear it.

"Really?" Jenny looked delighted. "That's the one I prefer. It felt ➤

right and I loved the neckline. I'd still like to go to the other boutique, but shall we go and have some lunch first?"

"Good idea."

She couldn't believe it when Jenny chose the very bistro where she had seen Carl and the blonde woman for the second time.

The bistro was tucked down a side road and Helen had only been there by chance. She'd taken a short cut through town to avoid heavy traffic on the motorway. A red light had brought her to a halt right in front of the bistro and through the window, she'd seen them chatting and laughing together.

"Helen, are you all right?" Jenny asked once they were sitting down. She looked worriedly at her friend. "You seem a bit distracted, a bit down."

Helen shifted in her seat. This was it, the moment she broke Jenny's heart.

"I didn't know if I should tell you, but I would want to know..."

"It's just that I've got something I need to tell you..."

"I've got something to tell you too," Jenny said excitedly. She looked as if she was about to burst. "Can I go first? It's so monumental that I can't keep it to myself any longer." She took a deep breath. "Carl has a daughter!"

Helen stared at her friend.

"A daughter?"

"Yes. I didn't tell you before because he didn't want anyone to know. He said it wasn't worth saying anything as he'd never had any contact with her. He was sixteen when his girlfriend got pregnant and although she kept the baby, her parents didn't want their daughter to have anything more to do with Carl.

"He was so young he didn't realise the consequences of relinquishing his rights and when the family moved away, Carl accepted he would never know his daughter and she would never know him.

"But he's never stopped thinking about her, hoping that one day she would try and find him. And then, a few weeks ago, she contacted him out of the blue. She's twenty-one now, and absolutely lovely. Carl met her by himself first and then introduced her to me. We got on so well that I've asked her to be a maid of honour at the wedding!"

A strange weakness came over Helen.

"You don't know how glad I am that you told me that." Tears of relief filled her eyes. "I saw them, Jenny, I saw Carl with his daughter and I thought – well, I thought he was having an affair. And I've been dreading telling you."

Jenny burst out laughing.

"An affair? I'm sorry, Helen," she added contritely. "I shouldn't be laughing, it must have been terrible for you."

Helen blinked back the tears.

"It was. At first, I didn't know if I should tell you, but then I thought, if it was me, I'd want to know."

"I'd absolutely want to know," Jenny said firmly. "You really are the best friend ever." She looked around for a waiter. "Shall we order wine? I think we could both do with a drink after that."

"I think I might need a bottle." Helen looked across at her friend. "I thought I was about to destroy your life."

"I'm sorry, Helen."

"It's not your fault, I shouldn't have jumped to conclusions. Don't tell Carl."

"I won't," Jenny promised. "Although he'd probably find it funny."

Helen sat back in her chair, able to relax for the first time in weeks.

"He must be ecstatic to have a ready-made daughter, especially when he'd given up all hope of ever seeing her."

Jenny nodded enthusiastically.

"He is. And you know what the best thing is? She looks exactly like him – tall, with the same black curls and the same dark eyes!" Ⓜ

CATHY BRAMLEY

A Perfect Pairing

It turned out that Mum's cheese and wine night made a perfect match in more ways than one…

After a scan through the post – a holiday brochure for singles, thanks for signing me up for that, Mum, a leaflet advertising babysitting services and a bank statement – I headed upstairs.

I'd been looking forward to a soak in the bath since dissecting fish heads with Year Twelve this morning. The counter-current gas exchange system in fish gills is a perennial favourite with the kids. Less so with me; the pungent smell of mackerel had followed me around all day.

With the taps on full blast, I added a squirt of bubble bath and left the tub to fill while I peeled off my pongy clothes in my bedroom. The cottage's old plumbing was so clanky and loud that I almost missed the sound of the phone ringing in the hallway below.

I'd been home for exactly thirty minutes, which meant the call was from Mum. I knew this because I'd once told her that after the noise and chaos of school, it took me half an hour to decompress when I got in and consequently I never answered the phone or doorbell during that time. As my little cottage was an appendage to the family home next door, she knew exactly what time I got in.

I turned off the bath taps and threw on my robe as I ran down the stairs. I could let it go to answerphone and call her back later, but then she'd probably worry about me and come knocking on the door. Besides, she was all I had left – and if I couldn't make time for my mum when she felt lonely, then who would I make time for?

I snatched the phone from the cradle just as my recorded message clicked in.

"Hi Mum."

She tutted. "It could be anyone."

"But it isn't, it's you. So," I said, perching on the bottom step. "What have you got to tell me?"

"Nothing special. I was supposed to be going out tonight with Josie but now her nephew has arrived unannounced. You know, the lawyer?"

Josie had been Mum's best friend for decades and it was down to her that Mum had a social life. She'd have turned into a recluse if Josie didn't drag her to line dancing, bingo, library talks and goodness knows what else.

"I do."

"Adam. Divorced."

"I remember."

"Lives in LA. Handsome chap."

"You may have mentioned him... once or twice."

She tutted again. "Less of your lip. Imagine working out there though, Polly. I bet the schools are amazing too, wall-to-wall sunshine and their own swimming pools."

"Hmm... and their own guns."

"What am I going to do with you?" she said with a weary sigh as if relieving me of my spinsterhood was her sole raison d'être.

I thought about the contents of my fridge.

"You can invite me for supper if you like."

"Oh!" That perked her up. "So you've no plans for the evening?"

Mum gave up work to care for Dad at home five years ago. He died two years later. I didn't blame her for not going back to her job as a part-time estate agent. That was up to her. But I did sometimes feel ➤

the weight of her loneliness, especially when Josie wasn't around. Matching houses with new owners had been the perfect job for her. She had, let's say, an "inquisitive nature".

"I was just about to have a bath. I'm a bit smelly. I can be ready in an hour."

"Perfect!" Mum could hardly contain her glee. "You can be my plus one instead of Josie. I'll call you at six-thirty."

I could have kicked myself. I'd fallen into her trap. Again.

"I can't," I said hurriedly. "I've got marking to do. Loads of it."

Supper with her was one thing, going out was quite another, because as much as I loved her, she had an annoying habit of trying to fix me up with a man wherever we went.

Any man. Anywhere.

"Don't you even want to know where we're going?" she said.

"We aren't going," I said firmly. "And I should go, my bath's only half full and it'll be getting cold."

Relieving me of my spinsterhood was Mum's sole raison d'être

"Please, love. I've got two tickets to a wine and cheese pairing thing. I was so looking forward to it, but Josie doesn't want to leave Adam on his own."

"How old is he, five?"

"He's a guest. It just wouldn't be polite."

"Mum, I'm sorry but I know nothing about wine –"

"That's the whole point! Neither do I!" she persisted.

"And it's a school night," I continued. "I'm teaching the reproductive organs of flowering plants to Year Nine tomorrow, painful enough without a bad head."

"Oh come on, humour your old mum. You can use the spit bucket thing. It's a shame to waste the tickets. Twenty-five pounds each!"

"Spittoon. Don't waste them, then – take someone else."

"Who, love?" she said reasonably. "Who else have I got?"

My chest tightened and in that moment I knew that I'd be going with her.

"OK, see you at six-thirty. But listen, please – under no circumstances are you to try and set me up with anyone, is that understood?"

Mum whooped triumphantly and put the phone down.

Mum parked the car and we got out. I felt a bit underdressed next to her now I was here. I'd only pulled on an old skirt and a jumper; she'd gone to town with full make-up and a dress.

"It's in the function room upstairs," she said as we crossed the car park. She looped her arm through mine. "Thanks for coming, darling."

"Thanks for inviting me." I squeezed her arm in return. "You're right, I'd end up working every night left to my own devices. And you never know, we might learn something."

We reached the door, headed inside and Mum gestured for me to lead the way up the stairs.

"That's the spirit," she said, beaming.

At the door, a man took the tickets from Mum, gave us name badges to put on and handed us a sheet of tasting notes. The room had a long bar dominating one side with a solitary barmaid behind it. The bar top had platters of cheeses and several cases of wine on it, along with rows of wine glasses.

"Find a table and take a red and white wine glass each," the barmaid told us.

Mum handed me a couple of glasses and I looked round for an empty table.

"Cooee! Marie, Polly, over here!"

Mum's eyes darted to mine.

"Oh look. Josie has saved us some seats."

I gritted my teeth. "You said Josie couldn't come."

"Actually, I never said that," she said over her shoulder as she marched towards her friend. "I said that she didn't want to leave Adam on his own."

For a second I thought about walking out. She didn't need me after all. I really did have marking to do and I could have done without a →

late night. Mind you, I was here now and without my car I was marooned. I sighed and followed Mum.

Josie stood up, her plump arms wide to hug us both.

"Marie! That dress looks gorgeous on you! And look at you, Polly. You look barely old enough to be in a pub, you lovely thing!"

"This is a nice surprise," I said, glaring at Mum as I submitted to Josie's cuddle.

"You see?" said Mum. "I knew she wouldn't mind."

"Good," said Josie, her round cheeks pink with excitement, "because I want you to meet Adam, my nephew. Adam, this is Polly."

I was bristling so much I couldn't even look at my mother, but beside me I heard her take in a deep breath. As well she might. The way I felt about her and her match-making shenanigans, it could be her last!

Josie waved her arm to one side and into my line of vision walked the famous, divorced, handsome LA lawyer that I'd already heard so much about.

"Pleased to meet you," said Adam, reaching for my hand. He lowered his voice. "Hope you don't mind me gate-crashing your girls' night out? It was a last-minute thing. My aunt said she had a spare ticket and didn't want to come by herself."

His grip was warm and just the right side of firm. Good looking, average height, slim build, Californian tan… his mouth was curved into a polite smile but his brown eyes held a hint of humour.

"Ditto," I whispered, glancing over my shoulder to where Josie and Mum were doing a terrible job of pretending to read the tasting notes while actually straining to listen in. "Ever since I spilt up with my fiancé, my mother has taken every opportunity to foist me on poor unsuspecting men."

"Same here," Adam whispered back. "Only not with men."

We shared a smile just as Mum grabbed my arm.

"It's starting!" She pulled me down into a chair beside her and Josie did the same to Adam.

"Welcome one and all, I'm Shane from the Winston School of Wine and I'll be your tutor tonight. Has everyone got a set of tasting notes there…?"

"You are in such trouble for this," I muttered to Mum under my breath.

"Oh, don't be a spoilsport. You need to grab life with both hands occasionally. You said yourself you'd be working every night if it wasn't for me."

"I also said no trying to set me up with any men."

She raised her eyebrows innocently and tuned into what Shane was saying.

He was telling us about the first wine while passing bottles of it around the room. A Sauvignon from the Eastern Loire Valley apparently, which thanks to its fresh green fruit flavours was a perfect match with the platters of goat's cheese accompanied by fig chutney and crackers which the barmaid was setting at each table.

My mother takes every chance to foist me on unsuspecting men

Mum was given an open bottle of wine and sloshed a bit in our glasses while Josie handed round the cheese.

Adam held a hand up. "Not for me, thanks. I'm a vegan. I'll have a cracker though. I've checked and these are fine."

"Since when are you a vegan? Anyway, there's no meat in cheese," said Josie, wiggling the plate under his nose. "Go on."

"It means he doesn't eat anything with a face," said Mum smugly. "Not even cheese."

Her friend cocked her head to one side, eyeing the goat's cheese curiously as if looking for facial features and then shrugged.

"Oh well, more for us, Marie."

"Vegan means that I have a solely plant-based diet," said Adam.

"Ooh!" Mum's eyes lit up. "Polly has the sex life of plants this week. Haven't you, love?" she enthused.

"Oh crumbs!" Josie choked on her wine. "That bad eh, Polly?"

Adam looked amused. Whether that was because of Mum and ➤

Josie's comments or because he really thought my sex life was that bad, I couldn't tell.

"I'm a teacher," I started to explain.

"I told him," Josie piped up.

"She's head of biology," Mum added.

"I'm acting head of science." I met Adam's gaze. "And what my mother means is that I'm teaching the asexual and sexual reproduction cycle of flowering plants this week. Well, tomorrow, in fact."

Adam grinned. "I remember it well. Do you still teach them about parasites and fungi too?"

"Yep. Can't wait for all the phallic mushroom jokes."

Mum spat out a mouthful of wine into the stainless steel container in the centre of the table. "Nice, that. Shame I'm driving," she said.

"I'm not. Adam is," said Josie, waggling her glass at Mum. "Fill her up. Don't be shy."

Mum gave a disappointed groan while Adam's stomach rumbled

Just then the barmaid came along with a platter of blue cheese wedges to go with the Riesling that was being passed around.

I speared a small piece onto a cocktail stick and ate it, and then immediately felt guilty when I heard Adam's stomach rumble.

"So how long are you back in the UK for?" I asked, offering him the basket of crackers. He took one and bit into it.

"A month initially. The law firm I work for want me to head up a new division. If I take the job, I could be back here permanently."

He chewed the cracker and then seemed to have difficulty swallowing it.

"Plenty of time for you two to get to know each other," said Josie.

"That would be nice, wouldn't it?" said Mum, looking at me while simultaneously nudging Josie.

Adam and I exchanged amused looks and I felt my heart skip a beat. He really was nice.

30

"It's a good opportunity," said Adam, after taking a small sip of wine. "But I do love California."

"Ah, but we'd love to have you home," said Josie, patting his cheek fondly.

"So what do you eat for meals, if you only eat plants?" Mum asked.

"It's easier than you think. I'm looking forward to a few decent curries while I'm back," said Adam.

"There's an amazing vegan Indian restaurant not far from here, I highly recommend it," I said. "I'll give you the name."

His eyes lit up. "Fantastic! Yes please. Unless, you… I mean…"

Mum and Josie's heads flew up and my breath hitched. Was he about to suggest a date?

"How's the Riesling?" Shane had been working his way round the room and had reached us. "Perfect match with the blue cheese, yes?"

Mum and Josie let out disappointed groans at the interruption.

Adam's stomach rumbled again.

"It's delicious," I said, taking Adam's hand. "But you must excuse us, Adam and I have to leave now. We have a dinner date at the Himalayan."

Adam stood up and helped me into my jacket. "Great wine choices, Shane. I'll be ordering some from your website."

"Excellent!" Shane gave Adam a business card and moved on.

"Do you have to go now?" said Josie, looking affronted. "Me and Marie were enjoying your company."

"And we haven't got to the reds yet!" said Mum. "There's a Rioja matched with Manchego, you love that, Polly."

"Not as much as I love curry." I bent down to kiss her cheek. "Thanks, Mum. I think you and Josie might just have made a perfect match of your own."

I smiled at Adam and led him out of the room. 🅜

ANNIE MURRAY

A Bit Of A Bump

It wasn't always easy being calm and professional when everything possible seemed to be going wrong

"A re you going to be long?" Chloe straightened up from bending to gather her bags and equipment from the car, and only then did the man shouting from behind the wheel of his BMW in the busy High Street see her uniform.

"Oh. Sorry." He revved off, in search of somewhere else to park.

"So you should be," she muttered, her already black mood darkening. It was bad enough having to work on Saturday, without her car breaking down and having to take Mum's embarrassing custard yellow one – and then some idiot yelling at her.

As if she didn't feel miserable enough already.

"Look, don't panic – take mine," Mum had said as she stormed into the house that morning after her car spluttered into silence.

Chloe felt like a little girl again with Mum trying to make her feel better. Her parents had been walking on eggshells round her since she'd moved back home, since she and Joe split up. Back home when she was almost thirty. It was never what she had wanted.

The workload was punishing, too. She was new to this area of the district and the list of patients seemed to go on forever. Next up was Mrs Bird who lived in the flats over the shopping centre.

She eyed the car. Not her best effort at parking. The back end wasn't quite in to the kerb. Still, it was a miracle she had found a space at all.

In the lift, she brushed down her uniform and dug deep inside herself to find her cheerful, kindly nurse's nature. There was a smudgy mirror in the lift. Her face, with slender, arched eyebrows, her brown hair neatly up in a pleat, stared sweetly back at her. It was amazing that she looked so calm when she felt so stressed and unhappy.

She might be the only person Mrs Bird saw all day. She had bad leg ulcers and probably never went out. The last thing she needed to see was a grumpy face.

Her knock was answered by a deep, smooth voice.

"It's open, dear – come in!"

Mrs Bird, a dignified lady with brown, beautiful eyes and soft white curls, was seated in her chair near the window, a book in her lap and her poor, swollen legs up on a stool. The living room of the flat was light and clean, carpeted in pale green. In a patch of spring sunlight lay a hairy black and white cat.

"I must say I'm glad to see your smiling face," Mrs Bird said, with such warmth that Chloe almost burst into tears.

She was an interesting lady who told Chloe that she had been in the Wrens during the war and that afterwards she had never married.

"Far too independent for all that." She made a comical, mock-scandalised face and Chloe laughed. "I find I get on better with moggies – like old Bosun down there." She nodded at the snoozing cat.

"But –" Chloe said. "Aren't you *Mrs* Bird? That's what it says here on my list."

"I most certainly am not," her patient said vigorously. "Never have been. People make assumptions. As if one can't possibly have survived life without having been shackled to some chap." She gave a deep chuckle. "Forgive me, dear. I'm sure you have some delightful beau in tow, lovely girl like you." ➤

33

"Nope," Chloe said. She smiled up at Mrs – Miss – Bird. She would have liked to linger all morning and hear her stories, but there was that list of patients. "Not at the moment."

Miss Bird's feistiness cheered her up and everything felt better as she descended in the lift. Until she reached the car.

"Oh no – this can't be happening!"

The left rear bumper had a whopping dent in it. She looked furiously round, but there was no one waiting to own up.

"Fancy not staying and facing me!" she ranted, unlocking the driver door. "What's Mum going to say when she sees that? I've caused her enough trouble already."

An even bigger cloud settled over her day. Driving to her next patient, Mr Giuliano, a bedridden man on the edge of town, all the negative things in her life swarmed about her.

She kept reliving that last, sad conversation with Joe, when they had owned up to the fact that after five years together, their relationship had run out of steam. The feelings were gone and only habit remained. They had been lying in bed, Joe's good-looking face, lightly freckled, his hazel eyes, welling up just as hers did.

"We're too young to settle for that, aren't we?" he said. "I know it's true – but I still don't know how I'm going to live without you."

They clung together and wept. She and Joe had known each other since they were fifteen, but they both knew that they were holding each other back. When they left the flat, handing back the keys and saying a quick goodbye – "Still friends", they said, hoping but not sure it would be so – it had felt as if half her life was being ripped away.

Once again, arriving at her patient's house, she pushed her own feelings away, wiped her eyes and became a nurse.

She dressed lonely Mr Giuliano's bedsores, drove to a Mrs Harper and sorted out her feet, then found the courage to pull in to a side road and call her mother.

"Oh, Chloe – I'm glad you've got in touch." Mum sounded flustered. "I was going to phone you but I never know if you're driving… I've had a man call me – rather odd. Said he had phoned the police because he had hit my car. I mean, it was nice of him really, not everyone would have owned up…"

"Well, he didn't stick around to own up to me," Chloe snapped, her pent-up feelings coming out.

"But you're all right, aren't you? That's the main thing."

"Yes." She imagined her mother standing in their kitchen wearing her anxious face. "I'm fine. I'm sorry, Mum."

"Don't worry. I'm sure it's just a scratch. As long as you aren't hurt."

Once again, hearing her mother's kindness, her eyes filled. She dabbed at them, careful to preserve her mascara.

"Still friends," they'd said, hoping but not sure it would be so

"Just get through the day and get home and then we'll sort it out. The man was really rather sweet, I thought."

She saw patient after patient, all around the town, eating an egg and cress sandwich in stages in between.

It began to pelt with rain. She hadn't brought an umbrella. Parking at the next patient's address, in a row of graceful old houses facing a field, she dashed to the door, her bag held over her head.

It was still raining when she finished with that patient. Just as she had switched on the wipers, pulled away and was getting up speed, a honey-coloured dog dashed out in front of her. She braked as the dog whisked past and into the drive of a house further along.

"Oh!" First she was horrified at the thought of hitting the animal. Then angry. What was the owner doing, letting it run about in the road like that? She could have killed it!

She eased the brake off again and moved soberly forward, peering up the drive into which the dog had run. Parked there was an old green Morris Traveller. She could see the dog, and a man hurrying down the drive. He must have heard the screech of brakes. ➤

"Oh no," she moaned. "Now he's going to have a go at me as well. And the dog's perfectly all right. This is all I need."

She put her foot down. In the rear view mirror, through the pummelling rain, she saw the man waving and shouting. He ran a few paces, then gave up as she tore off along the road towards her next patient, heart pounding.

When she finally got home, Mum laid a plate of spaghetti bolognaise in front of her and Chloe smiled, weary and grateful. This was the upside of moving back home!

"It sounds as if you've had a bit of a day of it, love," Dad said. He was just back from work himself. "But don't worry about your car. I called someone to fix it for you – and Mum's."

"I'm really sorry," she said, woefully.

As they ate she told her parents about Miss Bird. "I reckon she's got the right idea," she said, only half joking. "I'll get myself a nice little flat and a great big cat – although I'd rather have a dog."

She recalled him haring along the road and found herself laughing

"You can't have one with your job," Mum said. "Anyway – you're still getting over Joe. Just wait and see."

Chloe sighed and sat back in her chair, feet finally thawing out.

"At least I've got tomorrow off."

Chloe? Chloe!" She was just pulling on her jeans the next morning. She had heard the doorbell but was certain it was no one for her.

Her heart began to drum. Surely it wasn't Joe? She both wanted and did not want to see him.

"For you," Mum announced, standing back from the door as she came downstairs.

Outside, Chloe found a quaint-looking figure in a rather squashed brown trilby, a dark tan corduroy jacket and brown trousers. A round face looked worriedly at her, though the corners of his lips were upturned. Beside him stood a very large, pale dog, also apparently smiling.

"Found you at last," he said. "I've been trying to get in touch – about your car."

Chloe frowned. "What – you're the one who rammed it and didn't stop?"

The man looked abject.

"Thing was, I couldn't stop – not in all the traffic. There was nowhere to park and I had this one with me." He looked at the dog. "Then when I saw you later on... At least I assume it was you in that yellow peril..."

Slowly recognition began to stir. Parked at the end of the drive was a green Morris Traveller.

"That was your dog, in the road?"

"I tried to flag you down – I recognised the car. There aren't many that colour. Only you went off like a racing driver..."

Chloe recalled the man haring along the road behind her, coat flapping, and she found herself laughing.

"Oh – that was you, was it?"

He gave a little bow, a man both young and old at once. She just could not help liking him.

Later, once they had got to know each other, when her aching heart had healed and directed itself to him, she would call it "liking at first sight". Or second sight. Liking grew quickly.

"Actually," Mum said behind her, "it's my car you hit. Why don't you come in and bring that fantastic dog with you? I'm sure we could all use a nice drink."

The dog came closer and pushed its wet nose into Chloe's hand.

"That's Edna," the man said. "I'm Tom. We've both come to apologise. We must have given you a bit of a day of it."

"You did," Chloe said – and smiled, because he was smiling and she just couldn't help it. ⓜ

HELEN LEDERER

The Season For Love

Who knew that two free hot cross buns and a disastrous fake tan could lead to something so wonderful for Karen...?

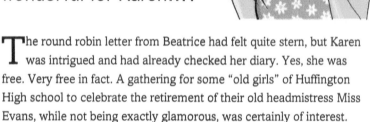

The round robin letter from Beatrice had felt quite stern, but Karen was intrigued and had already checked her diary. Yes, she was free. Very free in fact. A gathering for some "old girls" of Huffington High school to celebrate the retirement of their old headmistress Miss Evans, while not being exactly glamorous, was certainly of interest.

Karen had always liked Miss Evans. She had been the only teacher to encourage her creative writing, which had helped Karen enormously growing up.

She replied immediately and said she would love to attend. An exaggeration, but at least she would have somewhere to go next weekend, which made her feel better. Particularly as today was a bank holiday and the sunny weather was making her feel especially forgotten. All her friends appeared to have made plans and her jog around the park this morning felt especially solitary.

Was she really the only singleton in her postcode taking advantage of this precious sunny weather? It certainly seemed that way. The park appeared to be teeming with happy couples, and even the hordes of sulky teenagers appeared to be enjoying the sudden burst of sunshine.

Karen tried to look busy and self-contained as she jogged past some pretty clusters of tulips and a couple on a bench sharing a pair of headphones, but she knew she was lonely. If she hadn't stopped to buy a loaf of crusty brown bread at the Craft Fair on the way home, she would have spoken to no one for twenty-four hours.

Her last conversation had been the day before, when a fellow teacher waved her off with the cheery words, "Don't do anything I wouldn't do!" followed by a rather obvious wink.

The wink had been annoying, but it was understandable because she was the youngest, and it had to be said, most attractive, female teacher in the village school. She had taken to fibbing about a fictitious boyfriend, just to get people off her back, even if it was becoming tricky to know what fib she had told to whom.

Everyone in the teachers' common room assumed Karen was out on the tiles every night with a tall handsome boyfriend who had a red sports car and a demanding career. Sometimes she told them he was an osteopath and sometimes (when she forgot) she said he was in IT. None so far had commented on this anomaly.

It wasn't that she was lonely per se, she told herself, it was just that she hadn't made any plans for her bank holiday. That was all.

She hoped she hadn't been over-chatty to the man who had sold her the bread… but adult conversation had suddenly seemed very compelling. Especially when it was with a tall man who had curly brown hair and fashionably scruffy jeans. Teaching children all day, while rewarding in itself, had its limitations.

She recalled how nice the man's hands had been as he packed away her loaf in a brown bag, and how his brown eyes had been deep and smiley as he asked her how many miles she had "chalked up since sun up". His interest had made her blush slightly and she allowed herself a slight exaggeration.

"Three miles," she lied, pushing a tendril of red hair out her eyes while trying to look puffed and athletic at the same time.

"Three miles?" He nodded at her and smiled again.

She'd barely done half a mile, but he wasn't to know.   ➤

Unless he'd been watching her with a pair of binoculars from the stall. This thought worried her.

He'd included two free hot cross buns in the bag, which seemed a bit excessive. She'd only discovered them when she got home to unpack the bread.

They were delicious. Were the buns a message? Should she go back and suggest there'd been a mistake?

Worse, was it stealing? Would the police knock on her door to inquire about the missing two buns from Harry's Wholefood stall? At least she knew his name. Harry.

She pulled herself together. She was vexing unnecessarily. But images of Harry's smiley face kept distracting her. He really did have very nice hands, and was tall as well.

She had fibbed about a fictitious boyfriend just to get some peace

Pity about the apron, but at least it had been brown linen and was quite, well… *virile*… as aprons went.

She decided to email Beatrice again to ask who else was going to be at the lunch and could she bring anything food-wise. She needed a purpose. Anything to stop her thinking about the man with the buns and the nice eyes.

Beatrice replied in a slightly friendlier style this time and suggested that it would be "utterly wonderful" if Karen could write one of her poems to read out and that there was absolutely no need to bring any food.

The week went by quite quickly. Karen had taken another trip to the craft fair the next day, only to find that Harry's wholefood stall was never there on a Sunday. The organiser took great delight in informing her that a man as busy as Harry would rarely have time for his stall on a Sunday.

Perhaps there was a wife and children to attend to? Karen resolved to forget Harry completely and concentrate on writing a wonderful poem for Miss Evans, before booking a trip to the hairdresser, as well as a spray tan. The spring sun and abundance of daffodils in her front garden had inspired her. She wanted to appear sunkissed, even a little fragrant, as she read her poem celebrating Miss Evans' achievements.

The hair had been a success. Even Karen had to admit that soft curls were an improvement – she normally tied it back in a practical ponytail for school, but it felt quite nice to have her hair flowing around her shoulders.

The spray tan hadn't been quite as successful. She'd opted for a light blue sun dress and cardigan, which were both lovely, except for the tide mark of orange dye that had now spread across both garments.

Perhaps she should have listened to the instructions of the spray tan person? Was she supposed to wash it off or leave it on? She had left it on, and now it was feeling very warm and glowy on her skin.

The lunch was being held at a nearby country house and as Karen walked up the drive, she could see Beatrice with a clipboard directing people into the house with a dramatic wave of her arms.

A quick check in Karen's hand mirror showed that she wasn't just orange, she was now dark orange. She had to do something! She had to get the tan off, but how?

There were some wet wipes in her handbag, but she couldn't get past Beatrice without being seen. She noticed a path up the side of the house and quickly made a run for it. perhaps she'd find another door and preferably a powder room.

Suddenly she heard a familiar voice.

"You!"

"Oh," said Karen.

"Oh," he repeated softly.

"The buns… there were two extra hot cross buns in my bag," said Karen quickly. Maybe if they talked about the buns, he wouldn't notice the tan.

"I know. I put them in your bag. Did you like them?" asked Harry. Karen could see he was admiring her hair which was a good ➤

thing, but now he was also looking at her face, which wasn't quite as hopeful.

"Have you been anywhere?" he asked.

"What do you mean?" Karen opened her eyes wide.

"Well you seem different than when I saw you last."

"Ah. Yes... yes, I expect I am."

"It suits you," he said.

"Don't fib," said Karen and laughed suddenly.

Harry smiled at her.

"It was a spray tan last night. I think you're supposed to wash it off."

Suddenly, a young woman popped her head out from a door further along the path.

"Harry, quick. It's boiling over!"

Karen could see she was wearing the same brown linen apron. The woman noticed Karen and nodded at her in a friendly way.

Karen tried to return her smile, but she wasn't feeling it. The woman in the apron was very pretty. She waited.

"Anyway... I have to go actually, to this lunch."

"The lunch for Miss Evans?" asked Harry.

"How do you know?"

"I made the cake and...we're cooking your lunch, it seems."

Harry looked at her again and raised an eyebrow.

"So, we'll see you at the table?"

"We?" repeated Karen. She had to ask. She couldn't t stop herself.

"Debbie and I – she's helping out."

"Oh." They continued to look at each other. Debbie had given up and gone back inside to deal with whatever had been boiling over.

"Actually, I've got an idea, Karen –"

Before Karen could work out how he knew her name, Harry suddenly grabbed her hand and took her up the side path and through the door into the kitchen. Then he led her to a sink.

"Stand still here," he instructed and then very, very gently with a wet tea towel, he wiped away the worst of the orange tan.

Karen kept very still. She hardly dared to breathe. But she could smell his aftershave and fresh soap… she wanted to stay there for ever.

'There,' said Harry and stood back to admire his work. "No more orange," he announced.

"Still streaky?" asked Karen, wishing the soft stroking could have continued.

"Streaky is better than orange," said Harry with authority.

"True," agreed Karen and reluctantly tore herself away to join Miss Evans and an assorted group of fellow ex-pupils, all of whom were smartly dressed, and none of whom had put themselves at risk with a spray tan.

The lunch passed in a very pleasant manner. Miss Evans insisted on sitting next to Karen – Beatrice was on the other side of her – and it was a delight to discover that Miss Evans had remembered her well.

Karen's childhood hadn't been easy. She had grown up without a mother, and the creative writing had really helped her through her teenage years.

She was glad she had taken time with her poem. Miss Evans had meant a lot to her.

Harry grabbed her hand and led her through to the kitchen sink

As everyone commented on the delicious food, Karen wondered which dishes Debbie had cooked. Maybe she designed the menus? Or maybe they chose them together.

However, the memory of Harry and his gentle strokes with the tea towel had affected her appetite. She couldn't eat.

She reached for a glass of wine to settle her stomach. She had drunk two before it was time to read the poem.

There was to be a speech by Beatrice and the cake was to arrive just before Karen was to recite her poem.

Beatrice was beside herself with the excitement of the responsibility and kept checking her clipboard.

Karen was on standby when Harry and Debbie arrived at the table with the cake. The lights dimmed and Harry lit the indoor firework ➤

on the cake, while Debbie darted around the table handing out plates and cake forks. They made quite a team, thought Karen miserably.

Beatrice looked expectantly at Karen. This was her cue, but Karen couldn't bring herself to read the poem. She felt self-conscious.

Harry was busy cutting cake slices by now, but she knew he was looking at her out of the corner of his eye.

If only the pretty Debbie would somehow disappear...

Then, as if by magic, Debbie took out her phone from her apron pocket to look at a text. She nodded at it, then quickly gave Harry a hug goodbye before dashing off.

Karen was confused but relieved. She began her poem...

When she had finished, Karen felt aware of some hearty clapping, but her eyes were on Harry.

The room went very quiet. Harry was still looking at Karen with real intensity.

Even Beatrice began to sense there may be some other activity – apart from the items on her clipbard.

She took Karen aside, thanked her for the poem and then suggested that Karen might like to go and pay her compliments to the chef.

Much later, as Karen was helping Harry load his van up, she found herself asking something that suddenly felt very important.

"Why did Debbie have to leave so suddenly?"

Harry grinned at her.

"Come here," he said. He suddenly took her in his arms as he whispered in her ear, "Her husband asked her to come back and deal with my nephew."

"Oh," said Karen, trying not to smile.

"My sister helps me out when she feels sorry for me."

"And how did you know my name?"

"It said *Karen* on your jogging top. "

"Oh," she said again, and when she looked up at him, Karen knew that she had been looking for Harry for a very long time. Ⓜ

MILLY JOHNSON

The Magnificent Mystical Marilla

Marilla thought her sister didn't have the gift – or did she...?

©MILLY JOHNSON   ILLUSTRATION: ISTOCKPHOTO, SHUTTERSTOCK, MANDY DIXON

"So what do I do then?" said Cherice, trying to hold back her glee since today was going to be so exciting. Her big sister Marilla had a bug and needed to get back to bed.

Marilla was never ill, but today there was no life in her at all and extreme disasters called for extreme measures. Which wasn't good, of course, but what an opportunity it had given Cherice.

"Well, stare hard into the crystal ball," said Marilla. "Make it look as if you can see something really interesting and then choose from the list of stock phrases that I've written down for you."

Marilla felt bad about this because she took her profession as a fortune-teller very seriously. But the fair was moving on tomorrow and there was no way that she could afford to have The Magnificent Mystical Marilla tent unmanned. Her services were bound to be in demand.

If only Cherice had inherited the gift. They both came from a long, long line of Romany mystics but she hadn't shown the slightest inkling that she had any special powers.

She didn't even want to travel any more. She wanted to settle ➤

45

down in a little house with a nice man, get a cat and open up a floristry shop.

"Stick to generalisations," warned Marilla. "Over ninety per cent of people who come to the tent on Midsummer's Eve want to hear that they'll meet the love of their life soon."

Midsummer's Eve was all about finding your soulmate.

"Promise," said Cherice. "Now get back to bed. You don't have anything to worry about."

Cherice walked into the tent and felt a tremor of excitement at being in charge. No one would ever know that she hadn't a clue what she was doing. She really wished she could see the sorts of things her sister saw in the ball that had been handed down over the generations, but all Cherice ever saw were the reflections of things nearby.

She gave bucketloads of hope that Mr Right would be a corker!

She looked at the list Marilla had written down for her:

1. Most women like their men to be tall, dark and handsome.

2. All the women will have had bad luck with men in the past, but say that is about to change.

3. Mention that they need to carry some lucky heather with them wherever they go. The heather sprigs are under the table and are five pounds each.

On the list went up to point ten, which was written in very large capital letters:

UNDER NO CIRCUMSTANCES STRAY FROM THIS LIST.

Very straightforward… tediously so.

The day went swimmingly. The Magnificent Mystical Marilla's tent was proving very popular indeed, and Cherice really got into the groove.

She had even, by lunchtime, introduced the line "cross my palm with silver" and had now amassed a nice collection of coins that she'd keep to herself for her trouble.

She'd realised very quickly how many lonely people there were out there, all looking for the same thing as herself – stability and constancy and a drop dead gorgeous hunk. It felt really good to bring smiles to their faces by telling them that their own personal love-god was just around the corner.

The thing was, that by two o'clock she was becoming utterly jaded saying the same old stuff and had started improvising a little.

Not much, at first, just the odd detail... Tall-ish, rather than tall, and to a couple of women she said the man would have very brown/blue/hazel eyes.

She kept sort of close to her sister's script, but it was so boring – and it was surprisingly tiring, sitting on her bottom all day talking to people.

So when it was time for the final customer, Cherice thought that she had earned the right to finish off on a special high. Her last customer looked very much in the *I'm desperate for news about when I'll find love* cast, and so the least Cherice could do was give her bucketloads of hope that her Mr Right was going to be an absolute corker.

Sammy was indeed desperate for news about when she would find love. Going to see a gypsy at a fair showed how desperate she was, but her sister-in-law Kate had been to see the Magnificent Marilla two years ago when she was single, then last December, she had married into the family.

"She's brilliant," Kate had told her. "You must go – and buy the lucky heather, it so works."

"Come into my tent and take a seat," instructed the gypsy.

Sammy was surprised by her appearance.

"Oh! I thought you'd be older," she said, glancing at the poster which proclaimed that Marilla had twenty-five years' experience.

"It's all the travelling," answered Cherice, thinking on her feet. ➙

"It keeps me young, see. Please cross my palm with silver. The higher the value, the luckier you'll be."

"I've only got two-pound coins, but they're silver, in the middle, is that OK?" asked Sammy, hunting in her purse.

"Perfect," said Cherice. Ker-ching. She removed the silk cover from the ball and peered deep into the glass...

"I see much heartbreak in your past. You have been very unlucky in love," she said, sticking faithfully to the script to start with. She looked up to see Sammy nodding slightly. Even when people don't want to give anything away consciously, their body always lets them down, Marilla had once told her. She looked out for clues people couldn't help giving up – the blinks, the tics, the coughs, the nods – that told her she was on the right track.

"But don't worry," Cherice went on, "for I can see the man who is your soul-mate."

"Can you really?" Sammy beamed and Cherice was awfully proud of the size of her smile. She had made so many people smile today. She wanted to go out with a bang, wanted the last client not only to smile when she left the tent, but to bounce out as if there were mini-trampolines of joy in her sandals.

"Yes. He is very tall, red-haired and rugged."

Cherice hadn't given anyone a red-haired man today, or made them extra tall with craggy features. It felt like a nice change and much more convincing than the standard tall, dark and handsome.

"Oh my goodness," said Sammy, with a gasp of shock.

"Ringing any bells?" asked Cherice.

"Sort of," said Sammy, clamping a lid on her tell-tale signs of exuberance.

She's one of those that doesn't want to feed me info, thought Cherice. But it seemed as if she had taken a very lucky guess with Mr Red-Head.

"This man is in your life already, isn't he?" she prompted.

"Er, he might be."

"You didn't think he fancied you, did you? But he does. In fact, he really does. He's just very shy."

Sammy gave a little humph as if she disagreed on that one, but Cherice was cooking on gas by now. A quick about-turn was all that was needed.

"Oh yes, you might think he's a bit loud, but he doesn't wear his true heart on his sleeve. It's all show."

"Wow," said Sammy. "I never knew that. Can you see anything else?"

Cherice peered into the ball. "I see… he's very into sport." It was a safe enough bet, what man wasn't? "Something with a ball." If she'd got it spot on that the man was very big, then he was probably a goal-keeper – or a rugby player. She went with the latter. "Rugby. I see a rugby ball."

"Oh my," said Sammy, going red.

"He really does want to impress you. You should go and watch him play."

"Should I?"

"Definitely. He's bound to show

It was a load of twaddle, but it had given so many so much hope

off if he knows you're watching and play his best – and then his team will win and he'll feel very happy and brave, and that's when he will ask you out."

It was only common sense. Well, it would be if the big red-haired man actually fancied her in the first place. The woman was very pretty, so chances were that he would, though.

"Thank you so much," said Sammy. Her smile reached up nearly to her ears.

Mission accomplished, thought Cherice. Emboldened by her success, she added, "And if you want to buy some lucky heather, I have sprigs for sale for only five pounds. I see a lottery win for you too. Not a huge million-y one, but not one of those little piddly amounts either. Midsummer heather has magical properties, you know."

That part was actually true, since Marilla swore by midsummer heather picked at midnight.

Sammy, of course, bought a sprig of heather. How could she not? ➤

Her walk out of the tent was definitely a lot bouncier than her walk in had been.

Cherice sat back in the chair and sighed. She might have been talking a load of old twaddle all day, but she'd given so many women so much hope.

If only she really could see the future in her sister's crystal ball, but she couldn't. What fun it would be to foretell fortunes properly.

She was desperate to show her sister how much she'd earned today but she would conveniently forget to tell her about going off-piste with the last few clients, even though she was awfully proud of convincing that last lady to have such faith in her prophecy.

Her pocket was full of coins and she thought she just might go and treat herself and her sister to fish and chips from the little shop on the sea-front.

The following year the fair came back to the little seaside town. Marilla sat in her tent and told many women their fortunes. She was just about to close up and pack away when a woman came in. She seemed very surprised to see her.

"Is Marilla around?" she asked.

"Yes, I am Marilla," said the gypsy, a little confused.

"No. The lady I saw last year," said the woman, equally dumbfounded. "She had very blue eyes."

"Your sister told me the man I'd marry was a red-haired rugby player"

She meant Cherice. Marilla thought back, remembered being ill and her sister standing in for her.

"Er… she's finished for the day. I'm her sister, I'm just helping her pack up," said Marilla, thinking quickly. "Is there anything I can help you with?"

"Your sister told me my fortune. It was very specific. She told me the man I'd marry was in my life already and he was a red-haired rugby player."

Flipping Cherice! thought Marilla. She wasn't surprised, though. She had always doubted that her minx of a little sister could have stuck to what she'd been told to do. Marilla was only surprised she hadn't had a queue of women waiting for her when they rolled up at the town again to complain about duff forecasts.

"And she was totally right!" the woman went on. "I had no idea that James liked me, absolutely none. But I did exactly what she said and I went to a match to watch him play and his team won and afterwards he asked me out." She waggled her hand at Marilla. "And we're engaged.

"What's more, I bought a lucky dip lottery ticket and it won enough to pay for our whole wedding and a honeymoon. She was amazing! Will you please tell her the biggest thank you from me when you see her."

"I will," said Marilla with a dumbfounded smile. She would be seeing her sister tonight, before the fair moved on.

Last year, Cherice had gone to buy fish and chips for them both and fell instantly in love with the owner of the shop. She lived with him now in a cottage in this lovely seaside town. She had adopted a cat and was doing a floristry course at the local college.

What a waste, thought Marilla when the lady had left. It seemed that her sister really did have the gift after all. ⓌⓌ

JO THOMAS

Boyfriend For The Day

Poor Harry – this family picnic is about to throw up more challenges than simply pretending he's with lovely Lucia…

You said it was just a picnic!"

"I never said it was just a picnic."

Lucia stood beside Harry at the field entrance. Hedges lined the expanse dotted with clusters of ivy-covered trees. Running along one side was a small stream which children were attempting to dam with branches.

A strand of soft brown hair blew across Lucia's face as she looked up at Harry. He pushed his sunglasses up over his hair, slightly damp after his long bike ride, and stared at the packed cars arriving, tooting as they went.

"A family picnic, you said."

'They are mostly family. That's my grandfather's brother's family. And my cousins. Ciao!" She waved. "More cousins… I think."

"But we're in a field in Wales!"

"This is our Scampagnata. Our Italian families come together every year for this."

"Yoo-hoo!" A big-bosomed woman appeared from a bunting-festooned gazebo. Lucia pulled Harry towards her.

"Mama!"

"I'm not sure I can do this!"

"Harry, please. You have to help. Every year they want to know why I'm still single. This time they're going to set me up with a family friend's son, visiting from Italy. Please, Harry. If they think I'm with someone, they'll stop trying to marry me off to some 'nice Italian boy'."

"He might be nice!"

"He isn't. We grew up together, then his family moved back to Italy. He's annoying. Cheated at board games.

"Besides, I don't want a boyfriend. Not after Two Timing Trevor! My parents think they know best. I just want to pretend for the day. It's only because we're such good friends."

They'd hit it off straight away when they started working together in a Cardiff department store.

"Ciao, bella!" Lucia's mama, Maria, embraced her daughter.

"Mum, this is Harry. My, erm…"

Maria raised an eyebrow.

"Boyfriend." Harry tried to smile.

Maria eyed him suspiciously. The table behind her groaned with bowls of salad glistening with olive oil, piles of fluffy focaccia and florets of cured ham.

"And this is Enrico!" she announced.

Out from the gazebo stepped a tall, olive-skinned, smartly-dressed man.

"Lucia!" He kissed her and then shook Harry's hand.

"You're a lucky man." He nodded to Lucia, who suddenly looked very warm.

"Yes." Harry cleared his throat. "I am."

Enrico gestured to the gazebo.

"Come, meet my family. My mama has been cooking for days."

Maria laughed and nudged Harry.

"I started weeks ago!"

Lucia looked gobsmacked.

"Not the annoying git any more, then?" Harry whispered, before being swept towards the table. Maria positioned him firmly next to her. Enrico sat opposite, beside his mama, Donatella.

"Look at this spread, Mama!" ➤

Lucia picked up a plate and handed it to Harry. Maria beamed.

All around families greeted one another, Prosecco corks popped and cutlery clinked. Harry hastily pushed his rucksack, packed with Lucia's favourite cheese sandwiches, under the table.

"Give him more of my calzone," Maria instructed Lucia.

"Oh no…" Harry protested.

"You should try my Mama's calzone too." Enrico put some onto Harry's plate.

Enrico smiled at Lucia, who went pink.

Under the table, two small boys opened Harry's rucksack and pulled faces at the sandwiches.

"Try the meatballs. Mama makes them just how they should be," Enrico said.

Maria bristled.

"I'm sure yours are wonderful too, Maria," Harry said diplomatically.

Enrico added a spoonful to Harry's plate, which looked like Mount Snowdon.

"Mangiare!" both mamas commanded.

Enrico took a mouthful and smiled at Harry, who matched him bite for bite. Soon he was flagging, but felt determined to finish so as not to insult either mama or allow Enrico the satisfaction of winning.

"Magnifico!" Maria clapped as Harry sat back, stuffed. "Now, dessert!"

Both mamas produced deep dishes of dark, cream-topped tiramisu.

"You don't have to," Lucia said gently.

Maria, hearing her, looked horrified.

After two large portions, Harry looked beaten. The sun disappeared. Dark clouds rolled in and rain started to fall.

"Now, the tug of war!" announced a voice over the tannoy.

Enrico slapped his rival's back.

"Come on, Harry!"

Harry was on his feet, lurching towards the rope in the middle of the field, scowling at Enrico, striding out purposefully.

Facing Enrico, Harry was suddenly gripped by a desire to wipe the smug smile from his face. He couldn't bear it if Lucia decided to see Enrico again.

Actually, he realised, he couldn't bear it if Lucia wanted to see anyone else again.

"Avante!"

Harry stared intently at Enrico.

"Heave!"

Harry leaned backwards, pulling with all his might. But the ground was damp. Harry heaved, slipped, fell backwards and, for a moment, everything went black.

"Harry?" Lucia looked down at him.

Lucia. The loveliest person he'd ever known.

"Did we win?" he croaked.

"You did brilliantly."

"I wanted to make you proud," he said.

"And you did!" Tenderly Lucia wiped the rain from his face.

"So… Are you and Enrico… seeing each other again?" The words caught in Harry's throat. "Have I been dumped?"

"Never!" Lucia said. "Actually, I've quite liked you being my boyfriend."

"I liked being your boyfriend."

"We could always carry on pretending." She smiled.

"I'd like that." He smiled too.

"Let's see how our first pretend kiss goes, shall we?" She leaned down. "…For a pretend boyfriend, you're a good kisser."

"That's because I'm not pretending."

Grinning, Lucia helped Harry to his feet. He picked up his rucksack from under Enrico's chair. It was dripping. Inside was squashed calzone, four meatballs and a large dollop of tiramisu.

"Enrico's still an annoying cheat, then!" he whispered to Lucia, who giggled.

Maria hugged Harry warmly and tucked a tinfoil parcel under his arm.

"It's tiramisu. For later." She winked.

Harry had other plans. They involved Lucia rather than tiramisu – once he'd recovered from his two Italian picnics. Ⓜ

RACHEL HORE

Ups And Downs At Upalong Cottage

Now the kids were grown up, the cottage was their first holiday together, just the two of them…

I t was always left to Sally to book their summer holiday. Her husband Mike's excuse was that she was better at it – he'd just pick the cottage with the biggest TV screen and somewhere to keep his fishing rods, and wouldn't notice things she cared about like light and airiness and where to dry the washing.

This year she started thinking about the matter late and with a heavy heart, for it would be their first holiday without the children. Ben was on a work placement all summer before heading off for his second year at college, and Chloe was spending every spare moment with her boyfriend Jaz before starting university – exam results permitting.

"Let's go in September," Mike said firmly. "It'll be cheaper, and Cornwall's lovely out of season without the crowds. You've always wanted to see the Eden Project, and I could take a boat sea fishing." She gave him a look so he added hastily, "We'll do loads of things together as well, of course."

She cheered up when scrolling through properties within their budget on the self-catering websites, returning to the quaintly named Upalong, a tiny, white-painted cottage on a river estuary. There were two bedrooms, an enclosed back garden, and dogs were allowed so Coco, their elderly spaniel, could come too. The available dates worked perfectly, so she pressed the book button and paid the deposit.

The long weeks of summer crawled by. Results day came. Chloe had scraped into her chosen uni. Ben's placement was going well. Time to relax.

As the date of the holiday approached, Sally mused over a guide book and built a pile of novels to read. Two weeks by themselves! Perhaps it would be like the romantic early days of their marriage.

"You'll bring your new chinos, won't you?" she said to Mike when they were packing. "And a smart jacket. We could go somewhere nice for dinner, maybe."

"You're the boss," Mike said with a smile. He'd always been easy-going, Sally thought fondly. There were times when his diffident approach to life held him back, but she valued his gentleness. Chloe was like him, but Ben was more of a go-getter, like Sally's own father had been.

A late afternoon sun cast its golden glow over the cottage as they got out of the car after the long drive.

"So pretty," Sally breathed, admiring the pots of geraniums as Mike retrieved the key from under a window box. Her heart lifted as the door opened into a bright, clean hallway redolent with the scent of fresh flowers.

Coco's claws ticked across the pale wood floor. In the spotless new kitchen a basket of goodies awaited.

"Oh, how kind!" Sally exclaimed.

She explored the house from living room to master bedroom.

"Come and see," she called down to Mike. "The view's fantastic."

Mike clumped upstairs, a suitcase in each hand, and they stood together at the bedroom window to admire the stretch of river dotted with sailing boats and, beyond, a vast canopy of trees.

A glass of wine, supper in the friendly village pub, a good night's ➤

sleep from which they were wakened by birdsong, and the cares of daily life began to slip away. A day of glorious sunshine followed, with a walk along the river and a picnic lunch in the grounds of a ruined castle. Coco rolled on the lawns as though he was a puppy again.

"If this is what it's like to be empty nesters, I'm all for it," Mike sighed as they ambled home in the balmy early evening. "I don't miss Chloe and Ben squabbling one bit. Have you heard anything from them, by the way?"

Sally stopped to glance at her phone and shook her head.

"No, but there's no signal here."

"Thank heavens for that," Mike laughed. He was very disciplined about switching off from the hospital where he worked as a pharmacist, and could never understand why Sally, a counsellor who hated the thought her clients might need her, didn't do the same thing. "Shall we look into hiring a boat tomorrow? We could go upriver and look for kingfishers."

"If this is what it's like to be empty nesters, I'm all for it," he said

"Oh, that's a lovely idea." Just the two of them in the peace of the countryside.

"It really is magical here," her husband said. "It's the sort of place I'd like to retire to."

"Only twenty years to go," Sally reminded him with a laugh. "But I know what you mean."

The mobile signal returned as they reached the outskirts of the village. The ringtone meant Chloe.

"Hello, darling," Sally said affectionately into her phone. The only answer was a wail! "Chloe, are you all right? What's happened?"

"It's Jaz!" Another wail. Eventually Sally worked it out. Chloe's boyfriend had called it a day. The girl was desolate.

"If your brother's out at work all day you'd better come down here." Sally was concerned. "I'll check the train times."

She caught Mike's eye and Mike nodded, a sympathetic expression on his face.

"Thank heavens there's a spare bedroom," she remarked after Chloe had rung off. Her brain was already computing. There would be no boat trip tomorrow. Chloe had announced last week she'd become vegan and the village post office wasn't up to that. They'd have to find a supermarket in the morning.

Early the following afternoon they drove a dozen winding miles to meet Chloe at the nearest station. She stumbled from the train and collapsed sobbing into Sally's arms. Mike rescued an overflowing holdall and headphones she dropped on the platform and shushed Coco, howling in sympathy.

On the drive home the full story came out. Jaz had dumped Chloe because he wanted to start uni as a free man. Secretly, Sally wasn't surprised as they were too young to be serious, but he'd been Chloe's first steady boyfriend and she had been besotted. Now she gave every appearance of the break-up being the end of her world. Sally's heart ached as she comforted her.

Chloe rallied a little when she saw Upalong Cottage. She perched sorrowfully on the bed in the narrow boxroom with its flowery wallpaper, sipping a cup of sweet tea while Sally unzipped the holdall. Bottles of make-up and shampoo spilled out. Skimpy tops and underwear and a delicate party dress were scrunched up around half a dozen pairs of strappy, high-heeled shoes. No stout footwear, no coat or cagoule. Sally bit her lip, as she smoothed a tiny cardigan with pearl buttons into a drawer, then straightened.

"How about a walk?" she asked brightly. "It's lovely down at the river. There are swans with cygnets."

Chloe set down her mug, keeled over into a foetal position and covered her face with her hands. "I don't want to do anything," she mumbled and when Sally sat on the bed and tried to stroke her hair, pushed her rudely away.

Taking the hint, Sally retreated, closing the door softly and ➤

tip-toeing downstairs. She and Mike sat together at the kitchen table, not daring to stir in case Chloe needed them. On the wall the clock ticked lugubriously. Upstairs all was silent.

"I expect she's sleeping," Mike said in a soothing voice, squeezing Sally's hand. "She'll be all right."

"I suppose so," Sally said, eyes turning towards the ceiling. "I ought to be good at this, but it's different when it's your own child."

Chloe was a particularly sensitive teenager, her light bones, flyaway hair and huge brown eyes a magnet for those who like to bully and control. It had been a relief when Jaz had appeared on the scene. He was a kinder sort of boy.

"We'd best stay in, I suppose," Mike said.

"You can go out if you like."

"No, no."

They read quietly, alert to any sound from above, but it wasn't until six that they heard footsteps on the stairs, then Chloe appeared, her face puffy with tears. She consented to eat a little carrot soup.

After that she circled the garden, speaking frantically on the phone to one or other of her friends.

Inside, Sally and Mike half-heartedly watched TV, getting up every now and then to check she was OK.

It was a relief when their daughter finally went to bed. Exhausted by the day, they went to theirs.

At breakfast Sally's phone pinged. She read Mike their son's text. *I'm coming down. What's your postcode for the sat nav?*

A phone call later and she told Mike, "Apparently he's got some time off work. I've said we've no more beds, but he's bringing a tent. Do you suppose the landlord would mind?"

Mike shrugged. "There's the sofa."

They went and looked at it in silence.

It was wide enough for two to sit. Ben was a six-foot basketball player.

"He said he might come," Chloe said crossly when she arrived downstairs in pyjamas and heard the news. "I told him not to. He's doing it to annoy me."

"Why would he do that?" Sally said. "He asked me how you were."

Chloe made a moue and sulked the rest of the morning, then took Coco out for a long walk in her flipflops, declaring that she wanted to be alone. Sally waited, anxious for Chloe's return, but Mike went to investigate a fishing tackle shop down at the harbour.

Ben arrived late afternoon. Sally's heart swelled at the sight of her lean, sandy-haired boy as he uncoiled himself from the driving seat of the battered little car. He hugged both his parents and nodded at his sister, who curled her lip and flip-flopped back towards the house.

It had been lovely having a family holiday, Sally reminded herself

"Now come on, you two," Mike said vaguely as he helped Ben unload his gear. Camping equipment, wetsuit, hiking boots, Playstation. Mike's eyes gleamed as his son brought out a fishing rod from the back seat.

"Aha, good work, my boy. We don't need a licence apparently. They get salmon round here. Or we can go out to sea if we want mackerel."

Sally shot her husband a rueful smile and went indoors to make three lasagnes – meat for her and Mike, vegetarian for Ben, vegan for Chloe.

It was lovely having a family holiday, she kept reminding herself the following week, but the cottage was too small.

It rained one night and Ben's tent leaked so his kit littered the hall. Shopping and cooking took up precious time, even if everyone helped.

Mike and Ben, who had always got on well, made doorstop sandwiches and disappeared together to fish.

The day they brought back half a dozen mackerel Ben and Chloe had a fight about the ethics of a vegetarian killing fish. ➔

Sally devoted herself to cheering Chloe up with a trip to the Eden Project and a swim in the sea that necessitated the purchase of a new bikini.

In the evenings Ben and Mike played endless football games on the Playstation while Chloe messaged friends. Sally read a novel and silently plotted mutiny.

Then suddenly it was over.

Ben had to return to work. Chloe announced that a schoolfriend had invited her to stay. Sally and Mike helped pack up Ben's car and waved their children off.

Sally turned to Mike with a look of sadness.

"Well," he said, putting his arm round her. "Looks like it's just us again."

"I suppose we ought to clear up," Sally said in a dead voice.

"No, leave it. I've got a better idea."

The little motorboat chugged gently upstream. On either side of the river a tangle of trees grew down to the water. Pale shapes of fish lurked in the shallows. Then a darting flash of cobalt blue made Sally gasp with joy.

"There! Did you see it? A kingfisher!"

"I did," Mike said from the helm. They smiled at each other.

"You know, it's been great having Ben and Chloe, hasn't it...?"

"But very nice just being us again," she finished, laughing. "Shall we go out to dinner tonight to celebrate?" Ⓜ

PHOEBE MORGAN

The One After You

Widowed Kate is preparing to dip a toe back into the dating pool... amid a whirlpool of emotions

I haven't been on a date in ten years. There, I've said it. That wasn't so bad. I squint at myself in the floor length mirror, turning around so that I can check what the new dress looks like from the back.

My daughter chose it for me, insisted that the colour was "very me" and held up a hand when I moaned about looking chubby.

"Stop it, Mum," she'd said, smiling, "you look gorgeous." She'd looked so cheerful when she said it that I gave in and handed my debit card over to the cashier, trying not to let my smile drop even when I found out the price.

As if on cue, Alice bounds into my room now, phone in hand as usual, and snaps a photo of me in the dress before I can protest.

"Alice!" I say, half-laughing, but genuinely horrified at the thought of seeing myself on camera. "Put that away."

I turn to face her, taking her face in my hands. Her skin is so smooth, so youthful, and her eyes are glowing.

I know she's happy that I'm finally getting out of the house, doing something for myself. She worries about me being on my own, I know she does. But since Nathaniel passed away, I just haven't felt able to do any of it – the dating, the kissing, the dressing up.

It always felt like too much effort.

→

Besides, I'd thought to myself, who'd want to date me? I was fifty-eight, a widow with a seventeen-year-old daughter, a woman who was very set in her ways.

I suppose I'd got used to being alone.

"Are you sure you're going to be all right tonight?' I ask Alice for approximately the fortieth time this evening. She rolls her eyes, pads over to my dresser and begins rifling through the selection of earrings I have neurotically laid out on the surface. Beside them, the photo of her dad grins out at us – Nathaniel on the beach on a holiday in Norfolk, his hair windswept and his smile wide.

"Of course!" Alice says. "Sophie's coming over in a bit, we're going to watch a film or something." She turns around with a set of emerald green droplets. "Why don't you wear these? They'd go nicely with your dress, don't you think?"

At first I felt almost guilty but now I feel a little fizz of excitement

She holds them out and I put them on, staring at my reflection. Nerves are spiralling in the pit of my stomach; it's almost seven-thirty.

"Time to get going!" Alice says, giving me one last appraising look.

I feel a rush of love for her, my daughter – it's not as if Nathaniel's death was easy for her either. I know she misses her dad more than anything in the world, but she's wonderful at putting a brave face on it. Partly for my sake, I think.

Downstairs, I kiss her goodbye, breathing in her perfume and shampoo, the comforting familiarity of it. I shrug on my coat, wrapping my red scarf tightly around my neck. It's almost spring but there is still a nip in the air, and I'm grateful for the warmth of the soft wool.

Alice bought it for me – Christmas is always a difficult time for us both because it's when Nathaniel first became ill. Two years after the diagnosis, we said goodbye to him in his hospital bed.

Even now, the memories of the ward still give me nightmares, all this time later. What would he think, I wonder to myself as I approach the pub on the corner, if he could see me now?

"He would never want you to be unhappy," my friend Julia said to me, on the night we first talked about the idea of my dating. We'd been sharing a bottle of wine at hers, and I'd groaned when she'd reached for her laptop and pushed it in my direction.

"It's the way forward!" she'd told me. "Everyone's doing it! It's how people meet these days. Just because you've been out of the game for ten years doesn't mean everyone else has! Come on, here you go." She'd poured me another splash of wine and helped herself to a handful of crisps.

Two weeks later and here I am, about to go on my first date in ten years with a man I know only as *Oscar, 55.* To be fair to Oscar, the dating website didn't allow you to put much more than that – just a small section for detailing "hobbies and interests" which I agonised over for hours.

But I scrolled through photos of him, Julia cackling away beside me, and an hour afterwards he sent me a message. Since then, we have been emailing back and forth – niceties to start with, small talk that has gradually deepened over the last few days.

At first, I felt almost guilty for messaging him. But just in the last day or two, I've felt a little fizz of excitement whenever I see his name appearing in my inbox – a fizz of excitement that I realise I haven't felt in a decade.

The Eagle and Flag pub looks warm and inviting, its windows glowing golden in the dusky evening. I live in Bath, just up from the canal, and so it's only a ten-minute walk to get into town.

It was me who suggested this pub – I know the landlord, and it's a place I feel incredibly safe. As I'm about to reach the doors, a man, tall and straight-backed, brushes past me and I wonder fleetingly if he is the elusive Oscar.

But no – as I push open the door behind him I see him go to the bar and greet another woman, kissing her on both cheeks and quickly ordering a beer.

Flushing slightly, I turn away from him and make my way to a free table on the left-hand side. We said we'd meet on this side, and I told ➤

Oscar I'd be wearing a red scarf. Julia suggested I hold a red rose, but I put paid to that idea sharpish.

How's it going? Alice texts me, and I jump at the vibration of my phone, smiling to myself at her eagerness.

Only just sat down! I reply, just as Julia sends me a good luck message and a row of winking faces. Honestly. If I feel a bit pressurised, it's hardly any wonder!

"Kate?"

I look up from my phone, feeling my cheeks begin to burn, and there he is – a tall man with salt-and-pepper hair and a worn-looking brown coat. He smiles at me, and to my huge relief he looks exactly like his pictures – outdoorsy, the right sort of age, and – crucially – not wielding an axe.

"Yes," I say. "Yes, I'm Kate, yes, that's me." I force myself to stop – I'm babbling, as I do when I get really nervous. Nathaniel said he found it endearing.

"Oscar," he says, putting out a hand for me to shake. I suddenly feel as though I'm in an interview but grasp his hand in mine. It is warm and firm, with the hint of a callus on his right hand. Nathaniel used to get calluses after he chopped up the wood for the logs in the winter.

But I've got to stop thinking about him – I need to focus on the present.

"What can I get you?" he asks, gesturing to the bar with his other hand, and I fumble for my purse but he grins at me.

"No, no, these are on me. Merlot? Back in a sec."

While he's at the bar ordering my wine I surreptitiously look around for anything I might be able to check my reflection in – I'm hoping for a spoon – but before I know it he's back, setting down a large glass of red in front of me and an Aspall cider for himself.

There is a beat of silence between us and then I remember my manners.

"Thank you," I say, unwinding my scarf and taking a small sip of the wine – it is delicious, sliding down my throat like medicine.

"Just a little something to relax your inhibitions," Julia had said when I'd worried over whether to drink tonight or not. "A couple of glasses of wine won't make him write you off as an alcoholic!"

"Cheers," Oscar says, tipping his pint forwards to meet my glass. As he does so, our eyes meet – his are a grey, warm, ashy colour – and I feel it again, the zip of excitement.

As we settle in, I find myself relaxing a bit, the tension that had settled firmly between my shoulder blades slowly beginning to unwind. I catch the landlord's eye at the bar and he gives me a surreptitious thumbs-up, which makes me laugh unexpectedly.

"You have a good laugh," Oscar says, and I stop abruptly, because that's exactly what Nathaniel used to say. *It was one of the first things that drew me to you*, he always told me, *I heard it from across the room.*

The flicker of sadness must have shown on my face because Oscar looks a bit unsure of himself. His eyes are kind, and at once I feel awful that I might have made him uncomfortable. After all, no matter how nervous and inexperienced I feel now, he might be feeling exactly the same.

He doesn't take my hand. At the top of my road he pauses to look at me

"None of us really know what we're doing with this dating business, do we?" I say to him, and it breaks the tension, provoking a lovely grin that stretches across his face.

"You're right there," he says ruefully. "My daughter had to tell me what to wear tonight, can you believe?"

I smile back at him. "I can believe it. Because mine did too."

We chat for a little while about our children – he tells me Charlotte is nineteen, back from university for the Easter holidays. "She's studying medicine," he says, shaking his head in admiration, and the pride almost emanates from him as he tells me how hard-working she is, how dedicated.

"Her mother was a nurse," he says, and I detect the sadness in his voice even before he goes on to tell me about her death, in a road accident four years ago.

"For a while I was worried that Charlotte wouldn't make it to university," he tells me. "After Helen died, she was properly cut up. ➤

67

But the school were brilliant and she turned it around. She's at Exeter now. Graduates in two years' time."

"That's amazing," I say. "My Alice is looking at places now, trying to decide where she wants to be."

"Never easy when they go," Oscar says as he takes another sip of cider, "but you only want the best for them, don't you?"

"Of course," I say, "the very best."

Two hours later, darkness has fallen outside and I know I need to get back – Alice will worry if I'm later than ten-thirty.

At once, the lovely relaxed feeling dissipates at the thought of saying goodbye to Oscar. I don't know the etiquette – do I shake his hand again? Kiss his cheek?

"Shall I walk you to the top of your road?" Oscar says, and I panic for a second that he knows where I live before remembering that of course, I told him earlier in the evening.

He smiles at me and I nod, wrap my scarf back round me and we step outside.

The stars are out now, and as we walk he shows me them – Orion's Belt, the Saucepan, the North Star. He doesn't take my hand, but when we reach the top of my road he pauses and looks at me. He's taller than I am, and I feel a wave of nerves.

"I'd like to see you again, if you'll have me," he says gently, and in the light of a street lamp I catch a glimpse of uncertainty in his grey eyes.

Julia's words from the other night come back to me – *you've got to play hard to get, Kate! Treat 'em mean!* but that's not how I want to be. Oscar is a person, after all, a person just like me, trying to do his best after being dealt a difficult hand of cards.

"I'd like that very much," I say, and he solves the kiss-or-no-kiss situation by pulling me into a hug and promising to see me soon.

Back home, I get ready for bed. Nathaniel's photo smiles at me, and as I do every night, I touch it with my fingers.

Who was that? I imagine him saying, and I whisper back, "He's the one after you. You'd like him, my love." ⓜⓦ

LORNA COOK

The Lost Love

Of all the places to meet again the man I'd never been able to forget... fate seemed so cruel

I was late. Of all the days to be late, it really shouldn't have been today; the day of my friend's wedding.

I'd been travelling all day. The journey down to Cornwall had been hot and sticky and I had felt fairly confident before. But now, as I parked the car on the verge along with the other guests' vehicles, I was sure I was a bit of a mess – which was not the look I was aiming at for my darling friend Sadie's wedding.

Moving into the churchyard, I hastily hunched over to write the card on top of an old tomb.

She'd invited me by text, can you believe it? Surprisingly informal for a wedding. I checked the message to see what the groom's name was – but in her haste to organise her whirlwind wedding, she'd neglected to mention it.

I'm getting married, she'd trilled in her message. *You will come, won't you?* followed by the location, date and time.

Of course, I'd replied yes immediately. I'd leave a space for the groom's name and fill it in later, when I'd done some reconnaissance and found out who he was.

The heat was rising and plenty of guests were soaking up the sun, lingering in the grassy churchyard with its tilting headstones and bountiful but slightly thirsty-looking hydrangeas.

➤

I was relieved that I wasn't the only one who hadn't quite managed to take a seat inside yet.

There was no sign of the wedding cars, but the vicar popped his head round the large gothic door, beckoning us to take our seats.

I hadn't seen Sadie in so long. She'd gone away to work in Paris and what with one thing and another, our busy lives and jobs, we'd only managed to meet a handful of times.

She'd only got engaged six months ago, and all I knew about her intended was that he was "the most amazing man she'd ever met".

Someone called across the churchyard, "Is Chris here yet?"

Chris. I'd had a Chris once, but I hadn't told anyone about him.

My Chris had been a holiday romance that I'd kept all to myself – my delicious secret. In fact, returning to Cornwall where I'd met him, gave me a warm feeling of nostalgia.

We'd spent six weeks together working at a campsite through the summer, both of us on placements for tourism qualifications. I'd fallen in love and I was pretty sure he had too.

Thinking about it, I realised that no man since had ever stood a chance.

No one had matched up to Chris. Perhaps that's why I was still single.

We'd never said those three words *I love you.* We'd never dared. Because at the end of those heady six weeks, we'd kissed and said a heartfelt goodbye, realising that what with him living in Cornwall and me living in Suffolk, it really wasn't going to work. Not back then.

I'd had the best summer, though.

I look back now and know with certainty that Chris really was the most amazing man I'd ever met.

I joined the queue of guests as they filed slowly inside. I squeezed into a pew at the back on the bride's side, looking over at the order of service that sat in the lap of the guest next to me. I'd annoyingly missed picking one up.

All Things Bright and Beautiful took pride of place. I chuckled. I'd hated that one at school. So had Sadie, funnily enough. It must be her husband-to-be's choice, and I wondered about the push and pull of relationships where you agreed to a hymn you detested on your wedding day, just to please your other half.

I looked away from the order of service and then, with nothing else to do, looked back down at it again.

It was only then that I felt I was being watched. I have no idea if he had been watching me the whole time, or if his eyes had only just that second happened to glance in my direction. But I felt the draw of a pair of eyes on me and so I looked up,

I felt a pair of eyes on me and looked up towards the front of the church

towards the front of the church where, moments later, Sadie would soon be standing, saying *I do.*

That was when I saw him. I had to do a double take.

Chris. My Chris.

The one and the same.

I drew in a sharp breath. My mouth formed an "o" shape and I stared hard at the man I used to know. He was here – older, but very much here.

His face didn't carry the same expression of shock that I knew I was showing. Instead, he smiled, his warm eyes creasing at the sides in happy recognition. He remembered me. After all this time, he remembered me.

His smile turned into one of slight confusion as a frown slowly formed.

With horror, I understood the significance of where he was: at the front of the church. My Chris.

Although I had no real right to claim him as such. Not any more. Not after all these years. But I couldn't help but think of him as *my Chris.*

He put his hands in the pockets of his formal trousers and looked back at me as he reached his seat. But he didn't sit. ➤

There was so much I wanted to say. So much, suddenly, that I wanted to reveal. That I had loved him but that I'd never thought it would have worked. That I had been too young to really appreciate him and what we'd had, although fleeting.

When we'd spent that glorious summer together, he'd said, "If only we'd met when we were older," and I'd agreed, not quite understanding what he'd meant.

But looking at him, here, I do now. I know exactly what he was trying to say; that if we'd met on a glorious summer day in a Cornish church when we were proper grown-ups, with proper jobs and proper lives, we could have made the whole thing work.

There was the hubbub of a crowd in full confetti-throwing mode

Only we were doing that, weren't we? We were proper grown-ups now. So grown up, in fact, that one of us was standing at the front of the church, preparing to get married.

But it wasn't me. It was him… and he was marrying one of my oldest friends.

I struggled to believe it. How had the fates aligned to bring us together again? And like this?

It wasn't our fault. Neither of us had messed it up. Collectively we'd missed our chance. I tried to be happy for him, for them, but I couldn't be. I just couldn't.

And now I was going to have to watch them marry. I was going to have to sing hymns and sit through the service and then, oh God, I was going to have to go on to the venue afterwards and watch them sway to their first dance and cut their cake and kiss… How had they even met? Where had they met? And when?

I stopped thinking, interrupted from my spiral of self pity as the doors opened.

Music started: *The Arrival Of The Queen of Sheba.* Everyone rose and my heart sank. So this was it.

It was happening. I stood and sighed and glanced back at him, expecting to see his gaze directed towards the door, towards the imminent arrival of his bride to be.

He wasn't looking towards the slow stream of bridesmaids that led the way, resplendent in pale pink. He was looking at me.

He was smiling, but his smile was laced with disbelief. It felt too vain to think he might, just might, feel the same as me.

I cast him a slow, sad smile. I hoped it conveyed all the things I was thinking, all rolled into one. Loss, regret – and that regardless of the momentary surge of…something… I was feeling, that there was nothing that I would ever do to ever jeopardise the joint happiness of him and Sadie. I looked towards the bridal party walking towards us.

Maybe I could learn to accept it. Maybe one day I'd be able to visit them in their marital home, or have them round for dinner.

Would Sadie be moving home from Paris, or was he moving out there to be with her? It had been such a whirlwind romance, according to Sadie, I wondered if even they knew where they'd end up living?

Maybe, just maybe, I'd get a boyfriend one day and we'd all go on couples holidays together…

No. Absolutely not. I couldn't do that to myself.

I watched as the bridesmaids trailed past, painfully slowly. One step. Pause. Another step. Pause. I begged in my almost-frenetic mind, *Let's just get this over and done with.*

The bridesmaids had finally made it to the front of the church and had taken their seats in the pew. I closed my eyes tightly as I knew what was about to come.

I opened them as my lovely friend Sadie entered and paused for a few seconds. The effect was startling.

Sadie stood, just for a moment, in the doorway before moving on and as I took in her beauty – heck, even I wanted to marry her.

I looked back at Chris. I was going to allow myself one final look and then I was going to banish all these feelings and never allow them to creep back into my overwrought mind.

Chris was no longer looking at me. Of course he wasn't. Not ➤

when Sadie, gorgeous, unbelievable, beautiful Sadie had just entered the church.

Yet he wasn't looking at Sadie either. He'd lowered his head, his hand resting on the shoulder of someone seated in the front row.

Chris smiled a great, wide, reassuring smile at whoever it was, and slowly the someone else stood up; a man about our age in a formal suit. My mind whirred until I realised, with overwhelming joy, that it wasn't Chris getting married at all.

I smothered the shocked exclamation of pure, unadulterated happiness that burst from my mouth, eliciting frowns and a giggle from those in the row alongside me. But I didn't care.

The second man at the front looked white with nerves as he turned to face the congregation. He looked at Sadie, and I thought I saw tears of happiness in his eyes.

He mouthed something at her, and my friend mouthed it back. She caught my eye as she passed and gave me the happiest of looks. I returned it. It was all I could do not to spring out of the pew, into the aisle, and hug her.

She wasn't marrying my Chris. She wasn't marrying my Chris!

I watched Chris pull out a box and open it, checking its contents were still there. The sun glinted off the gold band inside and he snapped the box shut; a look of pride on his face as he readied himself for his duties as best man.

I'd never sung *All Things Bright And Beautiful* with more gusto in my entire life. I had an air of almost crazed happiness, and when the happy couple walked past and we all piled out into the heat of the skin-tingling Cornish sunshine I watched for him but couldn't see him anywhere.

We were directed to throw confetti; the photographer snapping away – and suddenly there he was, next to me.

It was as if the world had become silent and although there was the hubbub of a wedding crowd in full confetti-throwing mode around us, I couldn't see any of them, couldn't hear them. It was as if it was just Chris and I.

"Hello," he said, his gaze thick with meaning. He still had the same effect on me that he'd had all those years ago.

My voice faltered.

"Hello," I breathed.

"I never thought I'd see you again," he confessed. "Are you here with anyone?" He looked around urgently.

"No." I smiled. "It's just me. It's been just me for… a while. What about you?" I ventured.

He returned my smile.

"Same. Just me."

The photographer barked instructions from near the belfry tower and Chris and I did as we were instructed, obediently closing the gap in the group photo, inching closer together. His hand grazed mine and slowly I realised we were almost, very nearly, but not quite holding hands.

He looked down at me, giving me a questioning look, as if he was asking for permission.

I gave him an encouraging smile.

"We have so much to catch up on."

As the photographer clicked away in front of us, slowly, gently I felt Chris clasp his hand around mine.

He nodded. "We do." 🆆

RACHEL HORE

A Heartbeat Away

Busy career girl Hayley was worried about her father, but was his situation so different to her own...?

W as there anything else, Rory? Oh no, look at the time!" Hayley clicked "Shut down" on her computer and rolled back her chair.

"Nothing that can't wait," the young man said, shuffling his stack of papers. "I'll pull these figures together for Monday. Exciting weekend coming up?"

"Not really," Hayley said grimly, as she shrugged on her coat and freed a lock of auburn hair caught under the fur collar. "I'm late for supper with my dad tonight. What about you?"

She flashed a farewell smile at Rory, barely listening to his reply as she flew past him, scrabbling in her shoulder bag for the car key, only to have to wait at the lifts. She'd been in the office until after seven every night this week – no, not Tuesday, that had been a dinner with clients, the cosmetics group for whom her team had been doing market research. She'd not arrived home until midnight. She sighed. What a crazy life.

The lift pinged. Inside, she pressed the button for the car park. The door slid shut.

Drinks with the others at the Corner Bar, she remembered, that's what Rory had said he was doing. She wished sometimes that she had time to join them, but – she looked down at her expensive shoes – perhaps the team felt more at ease without their boss.

It could be a lonely life, she thought, as she edged her car into the traffic and drove through the dark, glistening streets towards the Victorian suburb where her father lived. She had friends, lots of them, but no time to see them. And now Dad was retired and on his own, and her mother in Newcastle with her new husband, she really needed to put him first.

Martin Shuckman pushed himself out of his armchair and went to the window, peering out into the rainy darkness. Still no Hayley. He reached to close the curtains, but his attention was caught by the house opposite. All its lights were on, and the front door stood open.

All day long there had been a huge van parked outside, and men unloading sofas and wardrobes, but now it was gone. As he watched, a lithe young man in jeans and a checked shirt came out. He was dragging a bit of old carpet which he dumped in a skip. Just then he looked across and must have seen Martin, for he grinned.

Martin nodded in response as the man crossed the road towards him. Martin went to open the front door.

"Hi, I'm sorry to disturb you." The young man was nice-looking, stood confidently, and his bluish eyes were full of good humour. "I'm Sam, Sam Westwell."

"Shuckman. Martin Shuckman." They shook hands. "How's it going there, Sam?"

"Fine, yes, I wondered if you could lend me a mug. I've got teabags and milk, but I don't know where the men put the crockery."

"Hang on." Martin went to the kitchen, picked a striped mug off the rack and gave it a quick wipe. As an afterthought, he opened a cupboard and selected a packet of bourbons.

"Cool – thanks," Sam said, taking mug and the biscuits. "That's really nice of you. See you soon, eh?"

Martin said goodbye and watched him go back inside his house and shut the door. He was about to close his own when he saw with ➤

relief Hayley's car drawing up. He waited as she parked, then stood aside to let her come in.

"Sorry, Dad." She sighed. "I know, I'm hopeless." There were fresh raindrops on her face. When she kissed him, her aroma of wet wool and soap brought a rush of love.

"You work too hard, that's the trouble," he commented as he drew her into the kitchen and poured glasses of her favourite white wine. "You need to learn to say no."

"It's not how it works these days, Dad," she said, sipping the wine gratefully. "Ooh, something smells good."

"Casserole au Père Shuckman. Bit of this, bit of that, splash of vino."

She giggled. "Mum could never get you to cook, could she?"

"What do you mean, my type? Clever, good-looking, charming?"

"But now I have to, I manage. It's only because you're here, mind. It's not fun catering for yourself, is it?"

He'd laid the kitchen table earlier and she sat down while he served out generous portions.

"No." They were both silent, each lost in their own thoughts.

Mmm, delicious," Hayley said finally. "So what have you been up to?"

"Well, let's see. I fixed the dripping bath tap, did some shopping, read the paper."

"Oh, Dad. Have you not seen anyone?"

"Apart from the woman at the checkout? Actually, yes," he remembered. "Someone came to the door. A young man. He's moved in opposite – you know, the house where the chihuahuas used to live? He wanted to borrow a coffee mug."

"Just someone who came to the door? I bet you don't even know his name."

"Yes I do. It's… Sam. I liked him. Your type, I thought."

"What do you mean, my type? Clever, good-looking, charming?"

"All those, I reckon." He laughed. "Seriously, though, you'd like him. I'm sure of it."

"I like lots of people, Dad. But it's you I'm worried about. You're too much on your own. And you're still wearing your wedding ring. Don't you see? It'll put women off, they'll think you're married."

"That's how I think of myself."

"You've been divorced two years, Dad. It's time you moved on."

"Move on. That's how people talk about it these days, isn't it? No one takes marriage seriously any more."

"Of course they do. You were married twenty-seven years. That's pretty serious, isn't it?"

"Yes. Yes! You're right, but what about you? Twenty-eight and still single. You don't make time to meet anyone – and one day it'll be too late."

"I'm establishing myself in my career just now. Once I feel the time is right…"

"When will that be, when you retire?"

She got up, nearly toppling her glass.

"I don't have to…"

"Hayley, sit down, please. Sit down."

She did, her eyes sparking anger.

"I'm sorry, my dear." He placed his hand on hers and could see her forcing herself not to pull away. "I suppose I'm still upset about your mother."

"And you blame her for me not finding a bloke?"

"No. Well… could there be some truth in that?"

"I don't think so, Dad. Look, if it makes you feel better I would love to find someone, but… it just doesn't seem to happen. I'm happy, really, though. I love my job."

"I liked mine, but they took it away."

'They didn't, Dad. It was voluntary redundancy, you remember. You didn't want to move to Eastbourne."

"Same thing. Early retirement. The scrap heap."   ➙

"You can still find another job, you know. Something part-time."

"Aye, I know, I know. I will do. When I get a bit of energy."

Later he watched her climb into her car and waved as she drove away. She was such a light in his life, and he wanted only the best for her.

As he stood in the doorway he glanced over the road to Sam's new home. There were no lights on. Sam must be out, or have gone to bed early.

Monday morning was a worse rush than usual. First Hayley had to take the car in for servicing, which made her late for work, then the managing director summoned her to an urgent meeting about workload, which meant she had to call the team together to prepare an update in readiness.

By five o'clock, when she was finally able to sit down with Rory to address the focus group figures he'd prepared, she felt she still had a day's work to do. It was then that her mobile rang.

"Sorry, Rory. Dad? Hello?" she said. Odd. Dad usually texted.

"Is that Hayley?" A strange man's voice. "My name's Sam Westwell. I'm your father's new neighbour."

"Is something wrong?"

"There's no need to panic, but he's had an accident. Can you come?"

"Dad's in the hospital. Something about an old carpet," she told Rory when she ended the call, shaking with shock.

"Hayley, that's awful. You must go. Don't worry – I'll carry on with these."

She grabbed her bag and felt for her car key then remembered.

"Oh no. Rory, the car's at the garage."

"I'll take you," he said immediately, pushing the papers away. "This job can wait. Your dad's far more important."

He looked so concerned that for a moment she wanted to hug him.

"I could just call a cab."

"No – I'll come. You look like you need some company."

Amazingly, there was an empty parking space close to Accident & Emergency. They found Hayley's father in a wheelchair in the fracture clinic, waiting for his ankle to be plastered. With him was a young man who introduced himself.

"And this is Rory. Thank you so much, Sam," Hayley said breathlessly. "Dad, what on earth have you been up to?"

"It's my fault really," Sam said. "I was loading some old stuff into a skip and your dad was helping."

Hayley was surprised.

"I was an idiot," Martin mumbled. "I tripped over my own feet."

His face was grey and etched with pain, but there was a sparkle in his eyes. He kept glancing towards the door to the hospital foyer, which puzzled Hayley.

Then it opened and a woman of her dad's age entered, holding a tray with three takeaway cups. She smiled.

"Sorry – I'd have got you both some coffee if I'd known."

Hayley noticed her fashionable jeans, neat, short blonde hair and how her pink jewelled earrings matched her nail polish.

"This is Jean, my mother-in-law," Sam said fondly. "She and Ruth – my wife – have been over today, unpacking." So Sam was married! "We're staying with Jean until our baby puts in an appearance."

> "I would love to find someone, but it just doesn't seem to happen"

"Moving house and having a baby at the same time is not to be recommended," Jean said, "but it's been lovely having Sam and Ruth. I've been on my own since my husband died, and I'll miss them when they go. Still, I'll no doubt be popping over to help with the baby."

"And when she wants a break from nappies, I hope she'll come and see me."

Hayley was astonished. Her dad, flirting!

"Careful," Jean warned, twinkling back at him. "I might just take you up on that."

➤

When Sam and Jean had gone and her father was in the plaster room, Rory and Hayley had a coffee in the hospital café. Rory had insisted on staying to give Hayley and her father a lift home.

"And I suppose it gives me an opportunity to say something, Hayley. I've been offered another job." He named a rival marketing firm.

"No!" She felt utterly dismayed.

"It's not a promotion exactly, but… well, it's difficult… working with you. You're a great boss, it's not that, but, don't you see…?"

She stared at him and suddenly understood. His sad expression was because of her! For the first time she saw how attractive he was with his springy hair and quirky smile.

"Do you have to take it?" she whispered brokenly.

"I think I do. Whatever happens."

His face said all she needed to know. She moved her hand across the table and touched his fingertips.

"Later," she said, "assuming Dad is OK, would you be free for a drink?"

"I might be." His voice was full of mischief. "It depends whether it's work."

"Mmm," she replied, mock-sternly. "I'm thinking of putting you on some extra duties." MW

CLAUDIA CARROLL

One Of The Girls

The idea of her mum moving in sounded great – until she transformed before Katy's eyes…

Poor Katy had a flatmate from hell. She'd dealt with less than desirable flatmates in the past before of course, but absolutely nothing compared to this.

"Sweetheart, are you there?" came an all-too-familiar voice from the bedroom as Katy's tummy shrivelled instantly to the approximate size of a walnut.

"Yes, Mum?" she called from the sink, where she was busy washing a mound of dirty dishes her mum had just dumped there earlier that evening.

"Can you help zip me into my leather trousers? I'm just having a bit of difficulty. And bring me in a nice chilled glass of Prosecco, while you're at it."

"Another one?" remarked Katy, rolling her eyes.

"Well – it is Saturday night after all," her mum called back cheerily. "As the song goes, let's get this party started!"

Gritting her teeth, Katy did as she was told, went to the fridge, poured the drink, then stuck her head around the bedroom door where her tiny shoebox-sized room was in total and utter disarray.

"Mum, what in God's name are you wearing?" she asked, shocked by what she saw. Because there on the bed, desperately trying ➤

ILLUSTRATION: ISTOCKPHOTO, MANDY DIXON

to wriggle into a pair of leather trousers so ludicrously tight that 1970s-era Tom Jones would have baulked at them, was her mother.

Meanwhile just about every other piece of clothing belonging to Katy lay strewn all over the floor, abandoned.

"I can't believe these don't fit me any more!" groaned her mum, almost ripping at the zip to try to get it to go up. "I've been a size ten my whole life. Don't tell me I've put on a few pounds now?"

"Mum, you can't go out like that," Katy muttered, deliberately banging the glass of Prosecco onto the bedside table. "And please take that crop top off, you look ridiculous."

"But I want everyone to see my belly button ring! It was agony getting it done, why would I go and cover it up?"

"I just thought, is this my life? And it's not. I'm only in my fifties"

"Mum, we're only going out for a few drinks with my friends, you're not going clubbing. At least, not again. Not after how you behaved the last time."

"Oh, listen to you," her mum said, sucking her breath right in and giving the tight zip one last tug. "All I did was have a few drinks and kiss that lovely Italian waiter. I'm carefree and single again and I can do what I want, can't I?"

"It was mortifying," Katy said with feeling, wincing just at the memory of that excruciating night. "That poor waiter was married and kept trying to tell you so."

"You know what? You're beginning to sound exactly like your father."

Katy was in the middle of scooping her clothes from the floor, but stopped in her tracks just at the mention of her dad. Her lovely, gorgeous dad... who was at home now, nursing a broken heart over all this. According to her mum though, this was all his fault and most definitely not hers.

"He's just such a fuddy-duddy," her mum had groaned at her, when she'd first broken the shocking news that, after twenty-nine years of marriage, she'd decided to up sticks and leave him. "So set in his ways. All he ever wants to do is to potter around the garden and head to the golf course at weekends. Never wants to travel or see the world now that he's retired – nothing.

"Anyway, I just looked across the breakfast table at him one morning and thought, *is this it? Is this really my life?* And you know what, Katy? It's not. I'm only in my fifties, I'm still young and I want to be young and feel young again."

That very weekend, she'd packed her bags and walked out on Katy's dad, leaving him wracked with guilt and bewildered as to what had brought about the sudden change in her. Not only that, but she'd announced she was moving in with Katy, giving her absolutely no choice in the matter.

Initially Katy had been all on for her mum sharing her tiny flat, even if it meant giving up her bed and sleeping on the sofa for the foreseeable future. *After all,* she'd reasoned at the time, *maybe I can talk her round. Make her see how much Dad loves and misses her and maybe even realise that deep down, she's happy and contented with him too.*

That wasn't the way it had worked out, however, and now – weeks later – Katy had to admit that this was a never-ending disaster. No sooner had her mum moved in than she started dressing differently.

"No more neat little suits and shift dresses from LK Bennett and Reiss for me any more!" she'd announced. "Take me to Topshop and let's get a whole new look for me."

The "look", however, turned out to be pure mutton dressed as lamb. Her mum was now parading around in torn jeans, a selection of crop tops and Converse trainers. Then there was the belly button piercing, the hair extensions that looked like matted rats' tails and the faceful of MAC make-up she was trowelling onto her face every day now.

All in all, this new look was more Barbie's Granny than anything else.

Not only that, but her mum had also decided that from now on, ➤

Katy's pals were all her new best friends too. She'd taken to inviting herself along on all of their nights out and initially her friends had been more than happy with this.

Now, though, the novelty was starting to wear a little thin – particularly when her mum would start misbehaving, drinking way too much and flirting outrageously with any man who looked her way.

"I don't get it," Katy's best friend Laura said to her. "Your mum never used to be like this. She was always so elegant and ladylike, and now it's like she wants to be a teenager again."

"Welcome to Mum and the mid-life crisis," Katy groaned, glad of the sympathetic shoulder to cry on.

As it happened though, that particular Saturday night, from out of nowhere a thought struck Katy.

Her friends were all gathered happily around a bar table, chatting away and enjoying themselves when another pal, Susan, joined them, sliding into a seat beside Katy's mum and looking very red-eyed and upset.

"Susan, are you OK?" Katy asked her worriedly.

"No," said Susan, as her bottom lip wobbled. "I'm not."

"Whatever's the matter?" Katy's mum asked.

"It's Derek," she sniffed, eyes welling up again at the mention of her ex's name. "He called over earlier to collect the last of his things from the flat and – oh Katy, he told me that he's seeing someone else already and we only broke up five minutes ago!"

"What?" exclaimed Katy, as her mum looked on, shocked.

"And not only that, but I checked on his Facebook page and he's posted a photo of the two of them in Paris at the weekend! And he knows I've always wanted to go to Paris…"

The girls all rushed to hug her with a chorus of "he doesn't deserve you" and "there's someone better out there for you, wait and see".

Then Deirdre piped up, "Break-ups are just the worst. Remember when Tom and I split after we finished college?"

"What happened?" asked Katy's mum, all breathless concern.

"Oh, it was a nightmare," said Deirdre. "We all went out to my favourite club to try and cheer me up, and there he was – with another girl from our class, out on a romantic date, if you can even believe that."

"Terrible carry on." Katy's mum shook her head disgustedly.

"Yeah – but when Gerry and I were dating," put in Laura, "that was the absolute worst of all."

"Tell me."

"We were together for a year and I really though he was The One. Then on Valentine's night, I got a bit suspicious when he never asked me out at all. So I called and called him and couldn't understand why I kept getting that foreign ring tone."

"Shocking behaviour. What you young women have to deal with"

"And what had happened?" Katy's mum demanded.

"Turned out he was in New York for the weekend – and he'd brought a date with him. They're engaged now and everything. Can you believe it?"

"I once got dumped via a direct message on Twitter," announced Gemma.

"Shocking behaviour," declared Katy's mum. "What you young women have to deal with these days."

Then Katy noticed her shake her head sadly and go rather quiet.

Seven a.m. the next morning, Katy hammered on the bedroom door. "What on earth's that racket for?" came her mum's muffled response from under the duvet.

"Come on, up and at 'em," said Katy, plonking down on the edge of the bed and pulling her trainers on.

"Don't tell me you're going jogging at this unearthly hour?"

"Yup. Certainly am, Mum. And not only that – but you're coming with me."

"Oh no. Do I have to?"

"You said you want to feel young again, didn't you? So this is ➤

all part and parcel of it. Now come on, up out of bed, it's time to get moving!"

The following week, Katy had been invited to a fashion party which was due to start at ten p.m.

"So come on, Mum, we need to leave the pub now, or we'll be late," she said.

"Oh darling, do we have to?" moaned her mum, rubbing her feet. "I'm just so tired already. And these wedge heels may be all the fashion, but they're killing me. I can barely walk another step."

"Not taking no for an answer, Mum. Grab your coat, it's gonna be a long night."

"I wouldn't get too used to being at home if I were you, though…"

Yet another weekend spent in the loudest, sweatiest nightclub Katy could think of and suddenly her mum was looking at her new life very differently.

"Oh Katy, I feel so awful!" she wailed the following morning, when she finally woke up and plodded her way to the tiny living room, where Katy was reading the Sunday papers. "And look at me, darling – I look about a hundred."

"I just made some coffee," answered Katy patiently. "That'll perk you up."

"I'm absolutely exhausted," lamented her mum. "And my head is pounding from the racket in that awful club. Did we really have to stay out till three?"

"But I thought you had fun?"

"Well," said her mum doubtfully, "don't get me wrong, darling. Your friends are all lovely and everything, but they're just so… *young*, that's all. So full of energy. I'm finding it hard to keep pace with you all. Do you know, I caught myself in the mirror at the club last night and you know what I looked like?"

"Go on, tell me."

"Like a sad, middle-aged women who just didn't belong."

"Tell you what," said Katy, getting up. "Why don't you and I go out for brunch this morning? My treat."

"Good idea," said her mum. "And later on, we can always catch up with last night's *Strictly Come Dancing*."

Then she broke off before adding wistfully, "Your dad and I always used to binge-watch it together at weekends. Then we'd have dinner and – now that I think about it – it was just all so cosy and comfortable and… well, lovely, really."

Katy and her mum had a gorgeous, leisurely brunch and if Katy did drag it out and dawdle for as long as possible, she could only hope her mum didn't notice. Later on that afternoon, as they strolled back to the flat, Katy asked her mum to go on ahead of her.

"I just need to – em – run to the supermarket to pick up a few bits for dinner later on," she improvised.

"A nice, quiet dinner at home and maybe then an early night?" Her mum smiled. "Music to my ears."

Kate skipped off in the direction of Tesco and allowed herself a tiny smile. Because maybe, just maybe, there was a happy ending in this for everyone.

Back at the flat later on that afternoon, Katy knew instinctively from the sound of voices coming from her living room that all was well.

Coming up the stairs to her front door, she even heard the welcome sound of laughter – then her mum saying, "Oh Brian, you shouldn't have. You really are too good to me!"

"Hi Dad," Katy beamed, coming into the living room and hugging her lovely dad, delighted to see him.

"There's my girl," he said, proudly hugging her back.

"And what's all this?" Katy laughed, seeing that every vase in her flat was now filled with cream tea roses, her mum's favourite.

"It's something I should have done a very long time ago," said Katy's dad. "Spoiling your mother rotten. Letting her know how much she means to me."   ➤

Katy's mum giggled girlishly from the sofa and flicked her hair.

"Thank you, Brian," she said, looking over at him fondly in just the way she always used to. "It's so good to see you. And I have missed you, you know. I miss my old life. Trying to be young again is just so… exhausting."

"Then come home," said Brian simply. "I could even take you right now, if you wanted? And we'd still be back in time for *Strictly*."

"Would you mind terribly if I did, Katy love?" her mum asked, but Katy just smiled back.

"Course not, Mum. And – for what it's worth – I think you're doing the right thing."

"I wouldn't get too used to being at home if I were you, though," warned Brian, "because I may just have a little surprise for you."

"Oh, I love surprises!" Katy's mum exclaimed, clapping her hands.

"You know how you always wanted to travel? Let's just say that this New Year is going to give us a lot to celebrate."

Her mum squealed and hugged him as Katy looked on happily.

A while later, when her mum was in the bedroom packing her things, Katy had a moment alone with her dad.

"Thank you," he said simply.

"For what?"

"For calling me earlier. For giving me a chance to slip into the flat so I could fill it with flowers. And for filling me in on the situation."

"Well, Dad, Mum wanted to be young and single again, so all I did was show her that life in all its facets." Katy shrugged. "The good, the bad and the ugly. Besides, I could tell how she was feeling, and that deep down she knew it really was the right time to go home."

"Home," echoed her mum, appearing in the bedroom doorway with a packed suitcase beside her. "What a lovely, lovely word." Ⓜ

ROSANNA LEY

The Flame Of The Rhumba

Dance classes are just what neglected Izzy needs to make her feel alive again… but what will happen in the rest of her life?

What happened on her birthday – or to be more accurate, what didn't happen – made Izzy think.

She took a step back to admire the shades of the new merino wool that had just come into the shop. Indigos and purples, ochre and forest green… she had a few customers who she knew wouldn't be able to resist.

She was fifty-five, and while this was not officially a big deal, it felt like it. Perhaps it was because they'd spent the last few years economising, saving up for a dream holiday. She had rather hoped it might coincide with her special day.

A holiday to remember – to Cuba, perhaps? That was her dream. Even David had admitted he was keen to see the classic American cars.

Izzy closed her eyes. White sands, a blue Caribbean sea, the crumbling splendour of downtown Havana, music and mojitos on every street corner…

"I was looking for a pattern for a baby's bonnet." A disapproving voice broke into her reverie. Izzy blinked. →

"Of course," she said politely. "Come and sit down and I'll fetch the pattern book."

On her fifty-fifth birthday there had been no surprise tickets for Cuba. There had been no night out at a fancy restaurant. Izzy had left the menu for the new seafood place in Lyme on the table for days, but David had failed to notice.

Instead, he came in from work late, armed only with a bunch of flowers that looked suspiciously like the garage variety.

> *"Feel the music. Let it stroke your senses, become your heartbeat"*

There was a card, hastily scribbled on and nothing like the cards he had bought her in the early days. They had been married for over thirty years. How had they so easily lost them, those early days?

"I'm sorry, love," he said. She noticed he looked tired and drawn. "I'll make it up to you. There's so much on at work..."

Izzy had shrugged. *So much on at work.* That had become David's mantra. And she'd had enough.

The following weekend David took her out and bought her "something she wanted". She chose an unsuitable red dress and ignored his raised eyebrows. The damage was done.

Their children, Nick and Stella, were grown up now and leading their own lives – albeit in that half-independent state involving trips home with bags of washing and requests for loans from the Bank of Mum and Dad.

For years Izzy had loved and nurtured them, put herself second to the needs of the rest of the family.

But from now on it would be different. She was fifty-five years old. She wanted something for herself.

The next day, she booked the holiday to Cuba.

"But we didn't even discuss it!"

David was aghast when she told him.

"If we'd discussed it," Izzy said, "we'd never go."

"It's just rather a bad time," David grumbled, checking his diary. "Why?"

But she didn't need him to reply. *There's so much on at work...*

Two days later, she enrolled for salsa lessons at the local arts centre. Cuba was about music and dancing. She needed to be prepared.

The class was run by Roberto. Of Spanish and Caribbean descent, he was tall, slim-hipped, in his early forties, with dark olive skin and chocolate-coloured eyes. It seemed to Izzy that he favoured her with a special smile.

"To dance the salsa," he said, "you must feel the music. Listen. Let it stroke your senses. Let it become your heartbeat. The pulse that drives you."

Let it become your heartbeat... It was heady stuff. Izzy closed her eyes and listened. It was stroking her senses all right.

When she opened them again, it was to see Roberto staring straight at her, a small smile playing around his full and sensuous lips. Goodness. She flushed. *The pulse that drives you.*

Every week she attended the class. Every week she learned a new step or two. Every week she watched Roberto demonstrate his expertise and she felt a small shiver deep inside. Everyone danced with everyone else.

But the moments of magic came when Izzy danced with Roberto. She could feel his hand resting on the small of her back as if it were branding her. *The pulse that drives you.* Indeed.

One night there was a social event and people were encouraged to bring friends and partners. Izzy asked David.

"I'm sorry, love," he said. "I have to stay late on Tuesday for a meeting. There's so much –"

"OK," she said breezily. "That's fine."

He glanced across at her, paused with his fork halfway to his mouth.

"You don't mind?" he asked.   ➤

"Oh, no," she said. "It wouldn't be your sort of thing anyway."

Because let's face it, David had no sense of rhythm – he couldn't dance to save his life – and if he wasn't there, well, she'd just have to dance with Roberto.

During the following weeks, Izzy forgot to re-order some chenille and sold some baby alpaca she was supposed to be keeping to one side for one of her regular customers.

She lost the thread of the conversation during her weekly "knit and bitch" session and she knitted three sleeves for the sweater she was making for Nick.

"You don't seem quite yourself these days, hon," one of her friends remarked. "Are you still getting those hot flushes?"

"Actually, no." Izzy stood up straighter – in the posture demanded for the salsa.

"What's wrong with you, Mum?" Nick asked her, as he examined a bag of washing that had turned a delicate and unexpected shade of pink. "You're all over the place."

Izzy attempted the same regal look that Roberto used on the dance floor.

"Actually, Nick, I've never felt better."

She couldn't stop thinking about Roberto. She thought of him in the mornings when she woke up, and in the evenings as she and David sat together watching TV. Thoughts of Roberto even crept into the middle of the night when she awoke to watch David, gently snoring, blissfully unaware of the visions in his wife's head. Of high cheekbones, white teeth and hypnotic dark eyes. Of shoulders pushed back like a matador's, of slim hips and a strong chest. Hands that could take you wherever they wanted you to go.

Let it become your heartbeat. Let the pulse drive you.

You have something special, Izzy," Roberto said to her one night when everyone was leaving after the session.

"Something special?" she echoed weakly. She couldn't admit to herself how she ached for praise from Roberto.

"Very special," he confirmed. "You are going to Cuba, yes?"

"Yes. In two months' time."

Dancing the salsa had changed her life, made her come alive. But how would she feel in Cuba – with David? Would it be the holiday she had dreamed of?

"In two months," Roberto said solemnly, "I can teach you the rhumba."

Izzy couldn't believe her luck, to be singled out in this way. They agreed on one-to-one lessons and Izzy could hardly contain her excitement. The rhumba – a dance of sensuality and desire.

> *There was a drumbeat, a plaintive melody. Izzy recognised a rhumba*

Over the following weeks, Roberto showed her how to shake and how to shimmy, how to swish her skirts, how to dance the rhumba.

It was intoxicating. Izzy felt young again, beautiful even. She was lit up by the flame of the rhumba and she didn't want it ever to end.

Although her home life with David seemed to have edged into the background lately, Izzy couldn't help noticing that he was working late more and more often – particularly on Thursday which used to be their "movie night".

One night when he came home late, she smelled beer on his breath.

"Have you been drinking, David?" she asked. "I thought you were at work."

He looked embarrassed. "Just a quick one on the way home, love."

Another Thursday she caught him humming. Humming? She'd never known David to hum. Then she noticed a smear of red lipstick on his cheek.

Izzy felt fear in the pit of her stomach. She didn't say anything. What was there to say? Middle-aged man stops paying attention to his wife and has an affair – probably with someone from the office. She could hardly bear to think about it.   ➔

The following Thursday he was late again. Izzy was distraught. She couldn't just sit around waiting for him. She left the house and drove to the Arts Centre where she knew Roberto was holding an intermediate salsa class.

She didn't stop to think what she wanted from him. She only knew that when he held her in his arms, all her problems seemed to disappear.

In the hall, Roberto was talking to a young woman with blonde hair and eager eyes. He didn't even see Izzy approaching in her tired old jeans and trainers, with not a scrap of make-up on.

"You have something very special, Karen," he was saying.

"Really?" The girl smiled up at him adoringly.

"So I wondered," said Roberto. "Would you like to learn to dance the rhumba?"

Despite Izzy's sadness – about David, about Roberto, about her own stupid gullibility – Havana was wonderful.

They explored the piazzas, the markets and the museums and walked along the Malecon, the sweeping promenade where the Classic American cars lined up to take tourists for a ride. They drank mojitos in the same bars as Ernest Hemingway, and walked up glamorous boulevards lined with restored baroque villas and glitzy hotels.

They would spend three days in Havana before being driven to Cayo Levisa, a tiny island where they could relax, snorkel, read and… *Dance the night away?* Izzy found herself thinking. She doubted that.

The first night in the club, David insisted she wear the red dress he had bought for her birthday. People were drinking cocktails, dancing, having a good time. And then there was a lull, a drumbeat, a plaintive melody…

It was a rhumba. Izzy recognised the rhythm only too well. She sighed. She'd had such huge hopes, but now she simply didn't have the heart for it.

"Come on," said David. He pulled her to her feet. There was a new kind of determination in his eyes.

"You don't even like dancing," she said. But at least he was making an effort. Perhaps he was being nice to soften the blow of what he was going to tell her. Perhaps he'd decided this would be their last fling...

Izzy stared at David. He was moving on the dance floor as if he knew what he was doing. He clasped her hand and drew it down like a wave. He kicked, he flicked, he shimmied and he twirled her around. OK, he was frowning in concentration – but he was doing it. He was dancing the rhumba.

"David!" Izzy was breathless at the end of the dance. "How did you...?"

"Thursday nights," he said. "A young woman called Juanita."

"Juanita? But what about –?" *Your affair,* she was going to say. And then she realised. There was no affair. Her husband was beaming at her. With love. Rather like he had in their early days.

"I thought it was about time I took a leaf out of your book," he said. "Work's not everything. And it's great, isn't it – the rhumba – when you know how?"

"Oh, yes," she said. *Let it become your heartbeat. Let the pulse drive you.*

Izzy had the feeling that this was going to be a holiday to remember after all. 🅼🅠

SARAH MORGAN

The Secret Affair

Torn between her love for Matthew and Jack, guilty Laura resorts to clandestine measures...

A re you absolutely sure you don't mind about this?"

"Mind? No way. I'm your sister. My job is to cover for you." Fiona put down her half eaten muffin. "I'm your willing accomplice. I wasn't sure you were going to go through with it, seeing as you're one big guilty conscience."

Laura wasn't about to disagree. These days she wore guilt like a cloak. "What if Matthew –"

"He will never know. When it comes to covert operations, I'm your woman. It's exciting! Call me Bond. Jemima Bond. You're 008. Licensed to thrill and be thrilled." Fiona gave an exaggerated wink. "I promise not to mention to Matthew that you're skipping out at lunchtime to have steamy sex with another man in a hotel out of town."

Laura felt her face heat.

"It isn't just about that. It's about being together. Spending time."

"I know. Stop worrying. You need this, Laura. You deserve it. Your life has been full-on for the past six months. You deserve a break and you don't have to apologise or feel guilty."

Fiona took another bite of muffin.

"And your secret is safe with me. You'll only be gone a couple of hours. Chances are Matthew won't even notice. He won't know you're a scarlet woman."

98

She wasn't. That was the problem. She'd never been the sort to flit between relationships. She'd always been a one-man kind of woman.

For her, it had always been Jack.

Until Matthew came into her life.

"You're right that I need this. Why can't I do something for me without feeling guilty?"

"Torn between two men. You're not the first person to feel that way."

"It's not as if I'm not happy with Matthew…"

"I know, but let's face it, he's not fulfilling all your emotional needs. Remember what that advice columnist told you. Seize the moment. Now go, or you'll be late."

She still couldn't believe she'd written to an advice columnist. Even less, that she'd admitted it to Fiona.

"She didn't tell me how to stop thinking about Matthew while I'm with Jack," she said lamely.

"If I know Jack, he'll take care of that. Did you buy that black dress? Show me."

Laura slowly unbuttoned her coat. A smile spread across Fiona's face.

"Wow. You're going to blow his mind."

"I hope so. It certainly blew my bank balance."

What had she been thinking?

"You asked for champagne?"

"Yes." That had been another chunk out of her budget, but she knew the only way she stood a chance of relaxing was if she had half a bottle of bubbly inside her. She felt an ache in her chest.

"They say there's no such thing as love at first sight, but the moment I saw him –"

"Matthew has that effect on women."

"At the beginning I used to stay awake, just so that I could look at him. There were nights when neither of us got any sleep because we –"

"Whoa!" Fiona waved a hand. "You love him. I get it. But you love Jack, too. That's OK."

"You make it sound simple." Laura looked at her helplessly. Fiona shrugged.

➤

"The way I see it, you're lucky. Most people can't find one person they love, let alone two. Make the most of it."

She'd picked a hotel a safe distance away. The thought of bumping into someone she knew made her break out in a sweat. They'd wonder what she was doing, sneaking into a hotel at lunchtime.

It was a good thing they couldn't see the sexy black dress she was wearing under her coat… or the sexy underwear under the sexy black dress.

Her heels tapped on the marble floor and she glanced around self-consciously. The hotel was luxurious, an oasis of calm and understated elegance a thousand times removed from the mundane, low-key life she led with Matthew. Was that why she felt guilty? Because even though she adored him, she wanted time with Jack?

Her stomach curled. He was upstairs waiting. There was no going back

A few people turned to glance at her and she felt her colour rise. Did she look like a woman who sneaked off at lunchtime to meet a man?

She approached the reception desk and her courage almost failed her.

"Jane Smith." She wished she'd picked something more exotic, like Persephone or Ariadne, but when she'd rung the hotel to book and they'd asked her name, she'd been tongue-tied.

Salome. Yes, Salome would have been good – especially as she was going to be doing the dance of the seven veils any moment now.

The seven veils of guilt.

The receptionist smiled and handed her a keycard.

"Mr Smith has already checked in."

Her stomach curled. He was upstairs. Waiting for her. There was no backing out now.

She walked to the elevator on shaky legs, trying to look as if spending her lunchtime in a hotel with a man was something she did all the time.

Taking a deep breath, she opened the door to the suite and paused.

He had his back to her and he was staring across the London skyline.

Then he turned, and the look he gave her stole her breath. In that moment, she remembered why she was here. Why she'd suggested this.

She'd missed him so much.

"Mrs Smith, I presume?" His eyes glittered with a hint of amusement. "I ordered champagne. I thought you might need to relax, as we've never done this before."

She'd met him at work, back in her single days, and in that first meeting, before they'd even exchanged a word, before Jack had even glanced in her direction, she'd been seduced by the rough texture of his voice.

It had been his looks that had hooked her, but his heart that had held her. And he'd held her whole heart. She'd never thought she could give even a part of it to anyone else.

She pushed thoughts of Matthew out of her head.

"I ordered champagne, too."

His smile transformed his face from serious to sexy. "Then we'd better get started. I don't want to waste a moment."

Her heart kicked against her ribs. She knew, even before he removed his jacket, that he was packing some serious muscle under that tailored suit.

He strolled across the room and opened one of the bottles.

She watched as he filled two long-stemmed glasses with a hand that was much steadier than hers would have been.

"Thank you." She took the glass from him and took a sip, aware of his gaze.

"Nervous?"

"Yes. I don't generally book hotel rooms in the middle of the day."

"And you're feeing guilty. Don't." His soft command made her bones melt. "He won't even know you're gone, Laura."

"I know." She took several swallows of champagne and felt the almost immediate effect.

Jack lifted his hand and brushed her hair back from her face, his fingers impossibly gentle.

➤

The first time he'd touched her, she thought she was going to burn up in the heat they generated together.

"For the next few hours you're mine, and mine alone. I've missed you. I've missed this."

Her stomach jumped with anticipation.

The surprise was not that she was here, but that she hadn't done this before. He was so very, very hard to resist.

What she and Jack shared was rare and wonderful. People went through life and never found what they had. That special connection. It would have been wrong not to embrace that.

He removed the glass from her hand in a deliberate movement and set it down on the table. Then he took her face in his hands, studying her as if memorising every one of her features.

"Jack —"

"Shh." He lowered his head and took her mouth, his kiss slow and skilled.

Her inhibitions fell away with her clothing, and for the next few hours she didn't give a thought to anything but this man, this moment.

Afterwards she lay dazed, warm and weak in the aftermath of pleasure.

"That was —"

"Yeah." He gave a low laugh. "It was. We should book a room more often."

"I need more practice. I don't think they believed I was Mrs Smith."

His phone rang and Laura tensed.

"Shouldn't you get that? It might be the office. It might be important."

Still, he was the boss, she reminded herself. If he didn't answer, no one was going to fire him.

"Whatever it is can wait." His arms tightened possessively. "Nothing is more important to me than you are."

He made her feel wanted. Special.

She'd wondered if it would feel awkward but Jack started to talk and soon they were laughing together and sharing their thoughts and feelings, just as they'd done before Matthew had arrived on the scene.

It wasn't until she was pulling on her clothes that she realised she hadn't given Matthew a single thought. Did that make her a bad person?

"I"m glad we did this."

"Me too." He buttoned his shirt without shifting his gaze from her face. "Maybe, one day soon, I'll even get you to myself overnight –"

"Not yet. I'm not ready."

He covered her lips with his fingers.

"Then we'll wait until you are. And in the meantime, we have this." He pulled her against him. "A hotel. Champagne at lunchtime. One of your better ideas. What made you think of it?"

Should she pretend she'd thought of it herself, or tell him the truth?

"I wrote to an advice columnist. Her name is Aggie, she lives in New York and she's brilliant. She writes a column called Ask A Girl. I told her about how torn I felt, how I was finding it hard to balance two relationships.

His arms tightened. "Nothing is more important to me than you"

"She said it was important for us to spend time together and that it didn't have to be overnight."

"I don't know who this Aggie is, but I owe her thanks."

This time it was her phone that disturbed them and immediately she was yanked back into the present.

Jack smiled. "Answer it. I've had you to myself for two whole hours."

The guilt was back. She felt torn.

"Do you mind? It's just that if Matthew needs me –"

She looked at the number. Her finger hovered.

"I love you." She blurted the words out in the seconds before she answered the call. "You do know I love you? I loved you before Matthew came on the scene, and I'll always love you."

"I know. That's why we did this, and why we'll do it again." His eyes darkened. "Take the call, sweetheart."

Her heart missed a beat. She picked up her phone, hand shaking. ➡

103

"Hello?" She was aware of Jack watching her the whole time, his expression inscrutable.

Some men might have been jealous of her close relationship with Matthew, but not Jack. He was totally secure in himself. And secure in their relationship.

She spoke for a few minutes, kept it brief, and when she ended the call he raised an eyebrow in silent question.

"He's fine," she said, relief melting away her anxiety. "And you were right. He didn't even notice I was gone."

Jack slid his arm round her and pulled her closer.

"Does that mean I get to have you all to myself a little longer?"

"Yes. He just woke up and he's a little grumpy, but Fiona says he's fine."

"Your sister is a wonderful babysitter."

"Yes. I know I've neglected you, but from the moment Matthew was born –"

"You fell in love with him. So did I. It's been a big adjustment for both of us," Jack said. "But we"re getting there. Fortunately love doesn't come in a measuring bottle. It's infinite. There's plenty of it to go round."

She was discovering that for herself. She didn't have to divide it into portions, because it never ran out.

"Once he starts sleeping through the night, Fiona says she'll stay over. We can go away for a night."

It was hard to imagine leaving Matthew for a whole night, but she was sure the time would come.

"Until then, sneaking off to a hotel with my wife works for me." His gaze dropped to her mouth and lingered there. "It's the most entertaining lunch break I've had in a long time. Happy Valentine's Day."

"Happy Valentine's." Happiness glowed inside her.

She was still smiling when he lowered his head and kissed her. 🅜🅦

MILLY JOHNSON

Odd-Bods And Supermen

When you grow up with someone, in your eyes they'll always be the same kid with the thick glasses or wild ginger hair...

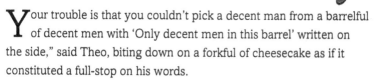

Your trouble is that you couldn't pick a decent man from a barrelful of decent men with 'Only decent men in this barrel' written on the side," said Theo, biting down on a forkful of cheesecake as if it constituted a full-stop on his words.

Lucy sighed. He was right. But then again, Theo was always right. He was the wisest person she knew and she felt blessed that he had been her best friend since they were at primary school.

They had gravitated to each other as the class outcasts. He, because he had glasses with a plaster over one eye and she because of her bright ginger hair. School became a more pleasant and less lonely place for both of them because of their friendship.

They'd started up the Odd-Bods Club when other misfits drifted to their friendship group: Sean who wore a hearing aid, Rick who was rather on the portly side and the willowy Karina, who towered above every other child in the school. Sean was now the headmaster of a school for deaf children, Rick was a prop forward for the England rugby team and Karina was an international model.

Theo hadn't done badly, either – he owned a string of barber's ➤

shops. His parents weren't too happy that he dropped out of his physics degree, and Lucy's support for him then helped him through a bad time.

Theo's parents didn't even turn up to the opening of his first shop, the ribbon cut by Vogue model and stalwart buddy Karina Malone. And despite a chain of barbers, a top-of-the-range Jag and a double-fronted country pile, they were still lamenting that he didn't have the letters MSc after his name.

Theo always saw a positive in a negative, though.

"If they hadn't been so critical, maybe I wouldn't have tried so hard to be a success," he'd told her.

Lucy had wanted to knock on their door and tell them how proud they should be of their son, who was flipping brilliant. One day, if she ever met the right man and settled down and had a son that turned out to be just like Theo, she'd feel blessed.

She'd dreamed of ripping off his top to reveal the Superman logo

But the chances of that were zilch. She might run her own translating business but she had no skill in picking boyfriends. No luck in finding the Superman she'd been hoping for ever since her teenage years.

Next time, she was determined to get it right. The man she'd set her sights on, she was sure, was a contender for The One.

Rick had met The One and was sublimely happy. Sean had met The One with whom he had a family now. Even Karina was happily engaged to The One, a Russian male model with cheekbones that could slice cheese.

Theo didn't seem in a rush to meet The One, though. *Better to have no one than a wrong one,* was another of his wisdoms.

"So tell me all about this Joe Pringle you're so in lust with," he said encouragingly after waving over a waitress and ordering two coffees. He and Lucy had a catch-up over dinner once a month. He might have been a busy businessman, but he always made time for his friends.

He was totally the perfect man: hard-working, kind, generous, smart, handsome. He ticked all the boxes for her – except the *does he make my heart beat faster?* box. Which was a real shame, because he was definitely The One material, with more than his fair share of Clark-Kentness about him.

His glasses, these days, were much more on trend though – with no plaster over the left lens.

"Well," began Lucy. "He's drop-dead gorgeous and moved into the flat above mine last week…"

"And you're already smitten?" tutted Theo. "Another love at first sight. Lucy, maybe it's time to take things a little steadier – play the long game, rather than the short one?"

"I'm not smitten," Lucy lied.

Joe Pringle was a personal trainer with bulging muscles. He looked like the sort of man who would rescue kittens from up trees and people from burning buildings. She'd had more than one daydream about him ripping off his work polo shirt to reveal the Superman logo on the garment beneath it.

"Oh, Lucy." Theo shook his head.

When Theo dropped her off at her home, Joe Pringle was just pulling up in his car – a sporty number with a personalised registration plate.

"Nice," said Theo, raising his eyebrows. It wasn't in the same class as his own, but he wasn't the type to disparage another man's pride and joy.

Lucy bounced out of the Jag in a rush and managed to collide artfully with Joe in the doorway.

"Hello," she said, eyelashes fluttering. "You've just moved in, haven't you?"

"Yep." Joe Pringle held out his hand and Lucy felt her heart leap as she shook it. "New to the flat and new to the town, so I know absolutely no one." ➙

"Well –" Lucy gulped because she wasn't used to being this bold. "You're welcome to have a coffee at mine, and I'll fill you in on the best places around and those to avoid."

"Sounds great," said Joe. "Now?"

Lucy wasn't expecting a yes, never mind one so immediate.

"I'll put the kettle on," she said, trying to sound cool – even though inside she was anything but.

So you and Joe Pringle are now an item?" said Theo at their next lunch, chinking his glass of wine against Lucy's in celebration.

"Yes, we are," confirmed Lucy.

Joe had asked her to dinner over that first coffee. She hadn't minded that he'd stumped up only half the price of the meal, leaving her to pay the rest. These were, after all, modern times and women shouldn't expect men to pay for them. And she hadn't commented that he'd had a starter, when she hadn't, and a fillet steak that cost twice as much as her pasta. It was fine.

And she'd not said anything when they watched TV in her flat and he'd used her new coffee table as a footrest. Or that he didn't volunteer to help her with the washing-up after she'd cooked them a meal. These were all silly little niggles and no one was perfect after all.

Her standards were too high, they always had been. She'd been waiting for Superman to appear all her life and he wasn't going to. Joe Pringle was the next best thing. Gorgeous and so strong.

He'd treated her to a display of weight-lifting in his flat. He had a whole wall of mirrors so that he could practise posing for the body-building competitions he entered.

"I'm really pleased for you," said Theo.

"I just wish you could find someone special too," said Lucy.

"Oh, I have," said Theo. "I'm going to take you to meet her when we've finished eating. She's got beautiful ginger hair – just like you."

Ruby also had luminous green eyes and it was quite obvious that Theo was besotted by her when he made his introductions.

"She's from the local rescue centre," he said. "Female gingers are special. Didn't stop someone leaving her in a box on the moors, though."

"She's fallen on her feet here," smiled Lucy, eyeing the box of cat toys and enormous climbing frame in the corner of Theo's swanky sitting room.

She liked cats. Mrs Wilby in the flat below her had an old male cat called Basil who always came to say hello whenever Lucy went into the communal garden to hang out her washing.

"Come on, I'll run you home," said Theo. He always opened the car door for her, made her feel like a lady. If only they fancied each other – but life, sadly, wasn't like that.

A week later, when Theo went to drop off a card and flowers for Lucy's birthday, he found her outside comforting the old lady from downstairs.

"Basil's got himself stuck up a tree in the garden," said Lucy. "Should we ring the fire brigade?"

"Let me see," said Theo.

Outside in the garden, a man who had to be Joe (bulging muscles as described) was holding a long wooden ladder up against the tree in question. Poor old Basil was perched

She'd been quite blind to how gulpingly gorgeous his eyes were

precariously high up on a branch, stretching a tentative paw out to purchase a solid platform but finding nothing.

"Oh great, Joe, you found a ladder," said Lucy with relief.

"I'll hold it for you while you go up," said Joe. "I don't do heights."

Lucy's mouth fell agape. Then Theo pushed past her.

"No worries. I'll go up," he said.

He climbed the ladder, which had been lying in the garden and was half-rotten with missing rungs. Even when he got to the top of it, Basil was still out of reach and Theo had to shuffle over onto a limb of the tree that might or might not have held his weight.

Lucy remembered that he didn't like heights either and pictured ➤

a school PE lesson when he was trying to control the shakes at the foot of the big ropes.

He still did it, though; he didn't want anyone pointing him out as the class wimp as well as making fun of his glasses.

Basil was frightened and didn't make it easy for Theo to grab him.

Somehow though, Theo managed to hold onto him as the cat squirmed and made "I'm going to scratch your eyes out as soon as possible" noises.

Somehow he manoeuvred himself back onto the ladder to make an unsure, slightly shaky descent to terra firma.

Once there, Basil made an ungrateful leap to the grass and disappeared through Mrs Wilby's cat flap.

"Pets, eh?" Theo laughed, rubbing at his clawed arm, his blue eyes crinkling behind his thick-framed specs and Lucy's heart gave a kick in her chest.

Just for a second there, she had a vision of Theo ripping his shirt open to reveal the Superman logo.

At their next early-bird meal, Lucy confessed that she and Joe Pringle were no longer together. Surprisingly, it wasn't to do with the fact that he'd bought her a *How To Lose Weight* hypnosis CD for her birthday.

"So how come you kicked Mr Perfect to the kerb, then?" Theo asked.

"It didn't feel right," said Lucy.

She didn't say that the sight of Theo stepping down the ladder with a wriggling, grumpy old cat in his hand had shifted something in her heart. It made her see Theo as others must see him – which wasn't the adult version of a geeky kid with a plaster on his glasses.

She'd always appreciated that he was kind, smiley, considerate and gallant but she'd been quite blind to how gulpingly gorgeous his blue eyes were, the width of his chest, his large, square hands, his really kissable mouth. Suddenly, Joe Pringle and his bag-of-walnuts body didn't seem half as strong and sexy as her old friend.

Theo had been on her mind so much since Basil-gate. It might make it quite awkward from now on, feeling this way about someone who thought of her only as a dear but dotty, idealistic, rubbish-at-relationships ginger pal.

"I'm sorry to hear that," said Theo. "I'm sure someone else will come along soon. Let's hope next time it really is The One."

"I think I'll give men a wide berth for a long time," said Lucy.

"Even me?" Theo raised his eyebrows.

"Even you," said Lucy, reaching for her wine, gulping at it.

"Well, that is a shame," said Theo.

"Only because *you'll* never find The One with me hanging around you all the time," she replied.

"Maybe I have already. Maybe I found her at school in the Odd-Bods club, the girl with the ginger hair – my best friend – and I've been hanging around ever since, waiting for her to find me," said Theo.

Lucy lifted her head to see him smiling and his lovely blue eyes fixed on her.

Superman's eyes. (MW)

EMMA CURTIS

Breaking The Rules

For Kerry, the only way to move on from her mother's death is to be a little rebellious…

The man in the grey wool coat drops two overstuffed carrier bags beside the door to the charity shop without acknowledging Kerry as she rummages in her bag for the keys. He runs off, jumping into his car and pulling out into the traffic with a screech of tyres.

Honestly, people can be so rude. Kerry rolls her eyes and carries the bags into the back for sorting on Monday when the full-time staff come in.

Out of curiosity, she pulls out a jacket. She holds it up, checking the label. It's expensive, from a shop she can't afford, and it also happens to be her size. It has a soft heather-green velvet collar and leather buttons. She slips it on and studies her reflection in the full-length mirror. It could have been made for her.

At five-thirty, Kerry switches the Open sign to Closed, locks the door and nips into the back room. Burning with curiosity, she rifles through the two bags, fingering silk and cashmere, leather and linen. Whoever these belonged to had a taste for elegance and the money to indulge it.

Kerry has thirty pounds in her purse. She puts it in the till and takes the new donations home. She knows such behaviour is frowned upon, but she can't resist. She's always been scrupulously honest, but it's only a little transgression, and no one need know.

Kerry began volunteering after her mother died, wanting to support the hospice that helped make her passing so gentle. During the week she works in a bank, a job she's held for eight years. Six years too long in her mother's opinion.

"If you don't ask, you don't get," she used to say. "You should be the manager by now, love. Be brave."

But she never had been brave, and now her mum has gone. Of course it's a relief that she's at peace, but Kerry misses her badly. They had been so close that moving on feels impossible.

And if she lacked confidence before, it's even worse now. Mary, her friend at work, keeps urging her to take a leap, but she's just not the sort of person who pushes for the things she wants.

That evening she empties the bags and tries on one garment after another. The silk skims her flesh, the cashmere is as soft as clouds. The colours suit her too – the deep bluey-pinks and cool summer reds bringing out the subtle roses in her complexion. A blue sequined evening dress enhances the colour of her eyes.

She laughs at herself and takes it off. When on earth would she wear it? She would feel a fool.

On Sunday Kerry gives herself a stern talking-to, picks out a pair of smart dark jeans and a snugly-fitting fine cashmere sweater and goes to the department store, just to see what it feels like.

The clothes she's wearing are a safe choice, but she's conscious of a lift in her spirits that transfers to the way she holds herself. For the first time in her life, she feels visible. The shop assistants treat her with deference even though all she buys that day are tights. Going out and about on Sundays in her second-hand finery becomes a guilty pleasure.

A few weeks later Kerry begins to feel as though she's being watched. At work, she tells Mary about it, laughing it off.

"It really is just a feeling. Perhaps I've got too much time on my hands now."

Mary looks at her with concern.   ➤

"You're missing your mum," she says. "It's understandable. If you took on a new challenge at work, it might help."

A new challenge? She couldn't see that happening any time soon.

Kerry walks down the high street towards the department store. She's wearing a camel-hair coat, belted at the waist, and feels like a movie star.

Until she hears it. The sound of footsteps that seem to echo her own.

She stops in front of a gallery window and pretends to study the paintings – oils of cows in a meadow. The footsteps stop. She spins round in time to see a figure dart down a side street, but whoever it was has vanished by the time Kerry turns the corner.

It's spooky," she tells Mary. "I'm beginning to think I may have a stalker."

"Have you actually seen anyone?"

"I'm not sure. I think I may have."

"It's probably just your imagination, Kerry. You're not really the type who gets stalked, are you?"

Kerry bristles.

"What type do you have to be?"

"I didn't mean it like that," Mary says hastily. "Don't take it the wrong way. It's just that you're a gentle, quiet-looking person, and your clothes don't exactly scream *look at me!*"

Flushing, Kerry glances down at her cheap blue cotton shirt. Quiet-looking! She'd show Mary.

The next morning, she chooses a slim black pencil skirt, a cream silk shirt and the jacket with the velvet collar. She blow-dries her hair and applies make-up, then grimaces at her reflection. She may have exchanged drabness for a touch of glamour, but she's still the same Kerry underneath.

She ticks herself off. She is a woman with options. Maybe she'll have a chat to her manager today, about her prospects with the firm. She pushes her shoulders back and lifts her chin. Maybe she will.

"Oh my," Mary says. "You look amazing. What've you done to yourself?"

Kerry flushes. "Just bought some new clothes… from a charity shop."

"You are clever! You must take me with you next time. Listen, I've heard there's a job going in management. Why don't you apply? It sounds absolutely perfect for you."

"I'll think about it," Kerry demurs.

Mary shakes her head.

"I'm not having that, Kerry. I've printed out the application form. You're not leaving this office until you've filled it in and taken it upstairs."

The train pulls into the station and Kerry gets off, pulling the camel-hair coat around her. She walks through the barriers and pops into the mini-mart to buy a salmon fillet and new potatoes.

As she's checking the best-before dates, a woman walks in. The hairs on the back of her neck rise. Is this her stalker? She doesn't appear to be buying anything, just studying labels while adding nothing to her basket.

Or could it be that young man in the hoodie, who glanced her way?

She is a woman with options. Maybe she'll chat to the manager

Uneasy, Kerry pays and leaves. It's dark and she walks briskly, growing more nervous once she's turned into the maze of less well-lit residential streets. She's certain now that she's being followed.

She lets herself in and slams the door, bolting it before she pulls off her boots. In the front room she draws the curtains, then peeks out. The street is still. At least, it was. A shadow moves, and someone hurries away.

Kerry arranges the food in the fridge and looks round the kitchen. ➔

Her mother has been dead for six months, the funeral and wake long over, but the house still smells of the perfume she loved, the garden still awaits her tender care.

Kerry knows she should make a decision about it but she's still taking her meals at the kitchen table where they used to sit, still watching her mother's favourite shows, curled up on the sofa.

"But he didn't ask. He just bagged everything up while I was out"

Her gaze rests on the figurine on the mantelpiece, the only thing her mother left of value – a seventeenth century shepherdess with an apron filled with tiny rose buds and a lamb beside her neatly booted feet. Her father had bought it at auction and given it to her mother as a wedding present. Secretly, Kerry doesn't like it, but she would never sell it.

She sighs. She doesn't need Mary to tell her she's going nowhere. She knows it only too well. Perhaps her stalker is the prod she needs. She shudders.

In bed, in the room she had as a child and teenager, Kerry is so scared that she can't sleep. She touches the rolling pin she's propped against the bedside table.

It's gone midnight before she nods off, but by then she's made a decision. She's going to the police. In the morning, she calls Mary to explain and gains herself a couple of hours.

"Oh and by the way," Mary says. "I'm so glad you applied for the new post. You've got an interview on Friday afternoon. Good luck."

It's still early and the High Street is quiet, many of the shops not yet open. Kerry walks along, catching glimpses of herself in the windows. She's dressed to impress and looks more confident than she feels. Is she doing the right thing? There isn't much to tell, after all; just a feeling; some footsteps; a possible sighting.

Whoever is shadowing her is back. She can feel it. After last night, she no longer thinks her mind is playing tricks; this is real. She walks faster, then stops to study the photos in an estate agent's window.

She sees the reflection of a woman, standing a few yards away, and her heart crashes against her ribcage. You read such frightening stories about stalkers.

The police station isn't far, but she takes a deep breath before turning and striding towards the woman, who looks like a rabbit caught in headlights.

Kerry is surprised at herself. She avoids confrontation. Perhaps it's the coat.

"Why are you following me?" she demands.

The woman stiffens. "I'm not."

"Yes, you are. And you've been doing it for weeks. Tell me why, or I'm going to the police."

To her surprise the woman's eyes well with tears. She pushes past Kerry and hurries away, her arms hugged around her body.

"Stop!" Kerry calls, running after her. "Please. I need to talk to you. Do you know me?"

The woman stops, looking Kerry up and down, her mouth trembling. "No. But that coat... those clothes..." She shakes her head and walks on, but Kerry blocks her path.

"What? I paid. I didn't steal them."

She feels a stab of guilt. She shouldn't have taken those donations before anyone else had a chance to look at them.

"He should never... I told him I wanted to keep them. I'm not ready."

Kerry remembers the man running up to the shop, dropping the bags. It had been curiously furtive; the action of someone who knew they were doing something underhand.

"They belonged to my daughter. She died five years ago." The woman dabs her eyes. "He said I have to move on. But he didn't ask. He just bagged everything up while I was out and took it away.

"I went to the charity shop on the Monday morning, but they hadn't seen any of it. They said he might have left it before the shop opened and it got stolen. But then I saw you in the department store." She ➡

looks at Kerry accusingly. "Why do you have my daughter's things?"

Kerry blushes.

"I volunteer there. I was opening up when he dropped them off. It was all so beautiful, and in my size. I paid for them – not much, I'm afraid."

She thinks about what the clothes have done for her confidence and strokes the lamb's wool with regret.

"I'll give it all back. I'm sorry."

The woman softens. "And I'm sorry I scared you."

"What was your daughter's name?" Kerry asks.

"Sophie. She was thirty-eight. She had cancer." Her voice breaks. "I miss her so. My husband… I know it's unbearable for him too, but it feels like he's driven a knife through my heart."

Kerry steers her into a café and buys tea and buns.

"My name is Kerry. Your daughter has changed my life. I'm so glad to have this chance to thank you and explain."

The woman, who introduces herself as Alice, listens and before long is giving Kerry interview advice.

They talk for an hour, but it feels like half that time. Alice has been a successful businesswoman and regales Kerry with her disasters and successes.

"You must keep the clothes," she says. "If they've made such a difference, I want you to have them. Sophie would too."

When Kerry walks towards the station to go to work, there's a lift in her step, but at the entrance she hesitates. She turns and heads home. She goes straight to the lounge, takes tissue from her mum's gift-wrapping drawer and smooths it flat. Her hands are shaking.

The shepherdess stands in pride of place in the charity shop window. Someone will pay a good price for her, and the money will go to the hospice. It feels right, and although Kerry suffers a pang for her mother's sake, she's glad.

Perhaps her small misdemeanour wasn't such a bad thing after all. Ⓜ

VIVIEN BROWN

Labour Of Love

The birth was imminent – and panicky auntie Jan was having to take charge

Jan watched her sister Laura lower herself into a deckchair in their parents' back garden.

The sun was baking hot, even though it was only mid-morning, and Laura had wisely positioned herself beneath the shady branches of the one and only tree, wearing a floppy hat and sunglasses, with a cool glass of lemonade in her hand and a book balanced against her bump.

"Are you all right there?" Jan could almost hear the ancient canvas of their dad's favourite deckchair groan as it stretched and bulged beneath her heavily pregnant sister until it was only an inch away from the grass beneath. "I could bring out a proper chair from the house for you."

"I'm fine. Don't fuss. And, to be honest, now I'm in it I'm not actually sure I could get out again. Not without help, anyway."

The baby was already several days overdue, and Laura's husband Dean was miles away, playing in a cricket match that he had insisted would not stop him from coming back to be right there at Laura's side if he was needed. Without a car, which was in the garage for repairs, how exactly was he going to manage that? Jan wished she could feel as calm as Laura so clearly was.

As Laura dozed in the sunshine, her dress straining to contain what looked like an over-inflated balloon, dangerously close to popping, Jan crept over and adjusted the hat that had slipped down over her sister's ➤

ILLUSTRATION: ISTOCKPHOTO, MANDY DIXON

119

face. A glance at Laura's book told her it was one of her usual romantic comedies. Comedy, indeed!

Since her cheating ex Peter had departed almost a year ago, Jan had found very little to laugh about, and no replacement boyfriend to offer her even a hint of romance.

That was the trouble with working in a small florist's with just three female staff, rather than a big bustling office like Laura's. And the men who did wander into the shop tended to be buying flowers for the women in their life, so not much hope there either!

She took Laura's empty glass inside and washed it up, along with the breakfast things her mum and dad had left before heading out for their Sunday morning supermarket trip. When she came back outside fifteen minutes later, carrying a tray of tea and biscuits, Laura was no longer asleep and her face was looking pinched and pale.

"You were fine just a few minutes ago. Are you sure it's not wind?"

"I think it's happening," she stuttered, screwing her eyes up tightly and trying to sit up. "I'm having contractions."

"No! You can't be." Jan felt panic sweep over her. She had never been good in a crisis. "You were fine a few minutes ago. Are you sure it's not just…"

"Wind? Indigestion? No, Jan, these are the real thing all right. You'd better start timing them, OK? Oh, don't look so worried. I'll be fine for a while yet. I'm not meant to go into the ward until they're five minutes apart.

"And you can drive me, can't you? If Dad's not back by then. I don't really want the fuss of an ambulance when the hospital's so close by. Ooh, is that tea? Just what I need."

Jan handed Laura a cup and checked her watch. Half past eleven. She took a few deep breaths. The last thing she wanted was to let her sister see how scared she was. Drive? She was shaking too much to drive. And what if the baby decided to pop out on the way?

"Should we call Dean?"

"Let's give him a bit longer, eh? He might not have had a chance to bat yet, and I'd hate to spoil his game."

Jan watched Laura blow on the surface of her tea and take a sip, then struggle to stop it slopping over into the saucer as she doubled over in pain again.

"Ouch. Didn't see that one coming!" Laura let out a long, slow puff of air. "How long was it since the last?"

"Only four minutes."

"Oh dear, I think baby might be in a hurry to arrive after all. Maybe you'd better call Dean –" She stopped talking. "Oooh, I think my waters have just broken. Grab your car keys, Jan. We're on our way to the labour ward. Assuming I can get myself out of this soggy deckchair, of course!"

B en limped to the door of the pavilion, where he'd been making sandwiches for the team, and waved his arms to catch his friend's attention. "Dean! Your mobile's ringing."

"Answer it for me, will you?" Dean called back from his position along the boundary, his gaze never leaving the ball that was flying through the air towards him. "I'll be right there."

Ben hobbled back inside, sat down and took the call. "Hello? No, this is Ben, Dean's mate. Can I pass on a message? Right. I see. No time to lose, then? Don't worry, he'll be there. I'll make sure of it."

There was a round of applause from the pitch and then Dean came in, wiping his hands down his once-white trousers, now smeared with grass stains. "Caught it!" he said, grinning. "That'll show 'em! The trophy's as good as ours. Now, what's happening? Baby started?"

"Well underway, by the sound of it. That was your wife's sister. Jane? Jean? I didn't quite catch her name, she was in such a flap."

"Jan. Lovely girl, but easily flustered. She works in a flower shop, says flowers are a calming influence, but I can't say I've seen much evidence of it! Right, I'll just let the lads know I have to leave and then I'd better hot-foot it to the station. Can't miss the big event, can I?"

"I think you very well might do if you have to hang around for a train, especially on a Sunday. No, I'll drive you. I've finished sorting ➤

out the food and the lads can make their own tea when they come in."

"You sure?"

"Of course. I've felt useless enough since injuring this knee. Not much of a twelfth man if I can't even get out there and take your place on the field, am I? And rushing a man to the birth of his son beats buttering bread any day. Just think, he could be a future England captain for all we know, and I'll be able to say I played my part… "

"Wouldn't that be something?" Dean's eyes shone with expectation. "I'd better get one of those mini bats and some soft balls for the garden, so I can start teaching him as soon as he can walk."

"Which is more than I can do right now! Good job I drive an automatic and I only need one working leg, or we'd both be on the train. Come on, grab your bag and let's go."

Jan winced as Laura squeezed hard on her hand and let out another muffled scream. They were in the delivery room, with Laura's knees pointing at the ceiling, and a midwife bending over the end of the bed.

"Won't be long now," she announced, giving them both an encouraging smile.

"But her husband still isn't here." Jan leaned over and gently wiped Laura's face with a damp cloth.

"Sorry, but babies come when they're ready, and this one is telling me he is."

At that moment the door flew open and Dean finally appeared, a hospital gown slung over the top of his cricket whites.

"Not too late, am I?" he said, strolling across to the bed as if he had all the time in the world and bending to kiss Laura on the cheek.

"Well, you've cut it fine, but I'd say you've arrived just in time." Laura pulled her hand away from Jan's and latched it onto Dean's instead.

"And, before you say a word, love, I may be flat on my back here but I don't want to hear any of your old 'bowling a maiden over' cricket jokes – all right?"

Jan moved away from the bed, smiling. She loved that easy way they had with each other.

"I think I should leave you now. This is a special moment for the two of you…" she began.

"Oh – here comes another one," Laura gasped, the sweat breaking out on her face again.

"What? Another baby?" Dean quipped. "We're not going to be having twins, are we?"

"This is no joking matter," Laura panted. "It's another contraction, and it ruddy well hurts."

"I know. Sorry." He wiped his hand over his forehead and swayed a little.

"Big push now," the midwife said.

> *"Don't tell Laura. She thinks we're naming him after my grandad"*

"And, Dad, if you want to just move down here and take a closer look… Here comes baby's head."

Jan opened the door to slip away. There was a loud crash and she turned back, startled.

Dean wasn't making jokes any more. He had fainted on the floor.

Ben gazed at the clock. "When I set off for the match this morning, I certainly didn't expect to spend my afternoon in a hospital waiting room."

"Me neither," Jan replied. "Sunbathing in the garden and one of Mum's roast dinners was all I had planned. And when I rang home, she said she's too excited to cook, so we're going to have to make do with sandwiches later."

"I've just left a mound of those back at the pavilion. Funny how life turns out, isn't it? A momentous day like this, and we celebrate with bread!"

He smiled. He had such a lovely smile, Jan could feel herself start to blush.

"Yes. And weak tea from a machine." She turned away, drained her paper cup and dropped it into the bin.

"Dean says you're a florist. I expect a lot of your bouquets end up here. Hospital visitors usually bring either flowers or grapes, don't they? Or both."

"Most wards don't allow flowers any more. Health and safety…" ➤

"Well, I didn't know that. Grapes it is, then! I'd better pop down to the shop in the foyer and see if they have any. And a card, of course."

"I don't think my sister's going to be thinking about food at the moment, and you should be resting that knee," Jan said, putting her hand on his arm to stop him getting up. "There's bound to be news soon. It would be a shame for you to miss it."

"You're right. It's exciting, isn't it? I've never been this close to a birth."

"Not as close as I was! To be honest, I didn't think I could do it. Stay calm and everything. I'm not known for it, you see."

"Well, I'm sure you did fantastically well. Rather you than me! And who fainted? Not you, but Mister Super Cool Laid-back Dean, that's who! Wait until the lads at the cricket club hear about that."

"What's that about the club?"

Dean's head appeared round the door. "Only its newest member has just been born. Eight pounds, three ounces. We're calling him Ian."

"As in Botham?" Ben grinned.

"Sssh! Don't tell Laura. She thinks we're naming him after my grandad."

Jan stifled a giggle.

"Mum's the word, mate," Ben said, touching his nose as if he was keeping the world's biggest secret.

"Not just Mum. Dad too! Can you believe it? I'm a daddy."

Jan hugged Dean, wiping a sudden tear away on his shoulder.

"Can we come in and take a peek?"

"They say not until visiting at seven."

"Right you are. We'll be back later then, won't we, Jan?"

"Oh, Ben, there's no need for you to hang around…"

"But I'd like to. And I think you said something about a Sunday roast. Care to join me in seeking one out? Find a nice pub somewhere?" He winked. "Much better than sandwiches."

A handsome man who made her laugh was asking her out for a meal. Jan felt a warm glow, as if she'd unexpectedly fallen into the first page of her very own romantic comedy. And she was not only the heroine – strong, calm and capable – but an auntie too!

The day surely couldn't get much better than that. ⓂⓌ

124

ISABELLE BROOM

The Key To A Girl's Heart

Would the fracas with the dodgy lock to a Greek flat help answer Bryony's prayers?

Bryony Clarke was a very long way from her comfort zone. If someone had taken her to one side even a month ago, and told her that she would soon be here, on a Greek island, completely alone, with her life as she knew it in tatters… well, she would have laughed in their face.

Nothing to laugh about now, she thought, sitting up on her sun lounger and scrunching her bare toes through the sand.

Bryony had been in a terrible mood ever since Leon had casually proclaimed over their Sunday roast that a) he did not love her any more and so would be needing his grandmother's ring back off her engagement finger, and b) that he was, in fact, in love with a vegan vlogger named Lara, who was twelve years his junior.

The howl of rage that Bryony emitted shortly afterwards was so loud, even the Yorkshire puddings had shuddered.

Leon moved out two days later, and a fortnight after that, the For Sale sign went up outside the house – their house. As if being dumped for a twenty-year-old "influencer" wasn't insulting enough, Bryony had been lumbered with the unenviable task of showing potential ➤

ILLUSTRATION: ISTOCKPHOTO, MANDY DIXON

buyers around what she had dared to think would be her forever home.

This was not how her life was supposed to pan out.

Bryony sighed, gazing down the beach to where a gang of skinny teenage boys were kicking a football around.

She had booked this trip at the last minute, buoyed by a combination of white wine and the shrill enthusiasm of her best friend. Ella had practically moved in since Leon had departed, and while Bryony appreciated the gesture, what she really needed was time by herself – space to stew and weep and puzzle everything through.

Bryony welcomed any triumph over her ex and his new girlfriend

Now that she was here in Zakynthos, however, so far from home and with six more isolated days stretching out ahead of her, she wondered if it had been the right decision. Ella's dire tea-making skills and perpetual TV remote-hogging was arguably enough to drive anyone out of the country, but then maybe that was the point. Perhaps her friend's entire nightmare-housemate charade had been a ruse to spur Bryony into action?

The marmalade dollop of sun that had warmed her limbs all afternoon was now beginning to sink behind the shifting dark-blue curtain of the sea, and in the far distance, Bryony could just make out the rounded turtle-shaped island she had spied from the plane.

Shadows stretched and twisted, and a light breeze lifted tendrils of her curly brown hair off her cheeks. Bryony could smell lemon, pine trees and the faintest hint of woody smoke… but all she felt was sorrow.

Leon should be here beside her. How would she cope without him?

The view had begun to swim in Bryony's eyes, and she allowed the tears to fall as she gathered up her things and pulled on her shorts. She missed him, that much was to be expected, but she also missed the security that came with him. Leon had always been the one in charge – of the bills, the DIY, the finances… all the important stuff.

It wasn't just that she wanted Leon in her life – she needed him.

In an attempt to distract herself, Bryony took out her phone, thinking that she would take a photo of the sunset. Instead, she found a message from Ella: *You had better be drunk and on the lap of a Greek man!*

Bryony rolled her eyes. Ella's instructions had been very clear. She had said, "You must sample as many Zakynthian delights as possible, and by that I don't just mean feta cheese."

A ride on a Greek donkey would apparently not suffice, either, and when Bryony had dared suggest it, Ella had replied with a remark so crude she'd clapped her hands over her ears.

Bidding a silent and somewhat reluctant farewell to the beach, Bryony made her way along the road towards Kalamaki resort centre, stopping off on the way to pick up bottled water, yogurts and three different varieties of crisps. Now that she no longer had a wedding to diet for, Bryony figured that she may as well welcome her old friend junk food back into her life. Leon used to love his greasy fry-ups whenever they came his way, but there was no way clean-eating Lara would allow *that* habit to continue.

Bryony tried to feel happy about the fact, remembering what Ella had said about getting over Leon being a one-win-at-a-time process. Anything that Bryony could use as a triumph over her ex and his new girlfriend – however petty it might seem – should be grabbed with both hands.

She had reached the block of apartments where she was staying and fished in her bag for her key. The ancient Greek lady who'd shown her to her room earlier had muttered something about the door, but Bryony hadn't paid much attention. She was too busy watching a tiny lizard scuttle up a nearby wall, thinking how much Leon would have liked it.

Now, however, as she slid the key in the lock and found that it wouldn't turn, she began to wish that she had.

"Oh, come on!" she hissed, gritting her teeth as she fiddled, ➞

fussed and faffed. It was no good – whatever angle she went in at, and however many variations of twisting she attempted, the door remained shut.

Resisting a strong urge to kick it, Bryony dumped her bag and towel on the floor and went to look for help. To her dismay, she found the office where she'd checked in locked, and the rundown bar area completely deserted.

Grumbling under her breath, Bryony began the whole process over again, this time cursing with gusto and kicking the door when she failed to gain access.

She was on the verge of more tears when she heard the buzzing sound of an approaching moped, and shortly afterwards, a man appeared on the path.

"Yassou," he said, noting her frustrated expression.

Bryony ran her eyes over his smooth tanned face, wide smile and messy black hair, and felt her cheeks flush.

"Yes, hello," she began, sounding ridiculously posh all of a sudden. What was it about English people? she thought. Confront them with anyone whose first language is not the same as their own and they automatically start talking like the Queen.

"Problem?" the man asked, even though that much was obvious.

"The door," she mumbled. "I can't get it open."

"Ah," he replied, looking at her with a mixture of pity and amusement. "Your boyfriend, he is not here?"

"No," she said, puzzled. "Just me."

The man frowned, then took the key from her and embarked on the same process of tinkering that Bryony had just exhausted, albeit with a few shoulder-shoves thrown in for good measure.

"Hmmm," he said after a moment, narrowing his brown eyes and lifting his hands in defeat. "Spasménos."

"Yes," she agreed, wondering what a "spasménos" was. She was just about to ask him, when the man pointed above their heads, gesturing at the tiny first-floor bathroom window which Bryony had propped open after her earlier shower.

"One moment," he declared, sauntering off in the direction of the bar, only to reappear less than a minute later carrying a plastic chair.

"You'll never fit," she exclaimed, jumping out of the way as he swung the flimsy piece of furniture round and positioned it under the window.

After clambering up, however, it became apparent that he was nowhere near tall enough to reach. Stepping down with a hearty grunt, he vanished again around the side of the building, this time returning with his motorcycle helmet, which he balanced on the seat of the chair with a flourish.

Her ex used to mock her and pick apart all her achievements

"Careful!" yelped Bryony, leaping forwards a fraction too late.

The man wobbled atop his helmet for a tentative second or two, then slipped violently to the left, bringing the chair down with him.

"Are you OK?" Bryony enquired, her words getting lost amid a volley of what could only be Greek swear words.

The man picked himself up off the ground, brushed the dust off his denim shorts and grinned at her. "Oops," he said.

A smile tugged at the corners of Bryony's mouth as she watched the man rebuild his makeshift tower, and this time she was ready to hold the chair.

After a few unsteady moments, his tatty flip-flops found purchase on the slippery surface of the helmet, and he pushed up onto his toes. Bryony looked on, feeling helpless, as he levered himself up with both arms. There was a gap of air between his feet and the helmet now, but he didn't seem able to go any higher.

"Shall I push?" called Bryony, reluctant to touch his hairy calves unless he gave her permission. His head was through the window now, but it looked as if only one of his shoulders would fit, and as she waited, his swearing began again in earnest.

Bryony dithered, unsure what to do. If she went to find help, she wouldn't be here to help if he fell. Then again, if she didn't, there ➤

was a good chance he would be stuck there all night. She was still mulling it over when she felt something wet connecting with her ankle and squealed in fright.

"What the –?" she began, letting out a sigh of relief when she saw the dog. "Hello there," she crooned, patting its soft, brown head.

An exasperated grumble filtered out through the window, and the dog, noticing the man for the first time, took one look at his flailing feet and jumped upwards, snatching one of his flip-flops and trotting away with it clasped between its teeth.

"Ela!" bellowed the man, and this time Bryony failed to stop herself giggling. She couldn't wait to tell her best friend that there was a Greek dog named after her.

She realised she was free to make as many mistakes as she liked

"Ela," he said again, and Bryony took a step forwards.

"You want me?" she asked, grabbing his foot to avoid being kicked in the face.

The man grumbled, and Bryony frowned as she heard him mutter something sour-sounding about women. It was all very well him blaming her, she thought – but he was the one who'd got himself stuck.

Leon used to mock her, too, and pick apart all her achievements. If Bryony cleaned all the windows in the house, he would point out the single smear she'd missed. When she surprised him with a candlelit dinner, he'd find fault with the seasoning of the meat. And the one time she'd managed to remove and clean the filter of the washing machine by herself, he had tutted and lamented to her that she'd most likely done some irreparable damage.

All of those times, Bryony had been meek. She had apologised and agreed that he was probably right – she was useless, and she was lucky to have someone like him in her life, someone capable, someone who looked after her.

As she stood, watching her so-called saviour suspended and

squirming above her, it dawned on Bryony that she no longer had to feel ashamed. Leon had left and taken his affection and support away with him, but what had also gone was all his disdain and disgruntlement. She was free to make as many mistakes as she liked now, without fear of retribution – or worse, bullying.

All this time she had been so fretful about how she would cope without him, when what she should have been focusing on were the benefits of his departure. In Leon's eyes, she was a screw-up – but in her own, she could be anything she wanted to be.

The man emitted a growl and tried once more to lever himself through the window. His T-shirt had ridden up, and Bryony could see an untidy pattern of thick black hair on his back.

"Right, come on," she instructed, surprised by the weight of authority in her tone. "Time to get down."

"No!" he thundered, cursing as his other flip-flop fell off. He was now attempting to climb higher up the wall by placing his bare feet against it, and his bottom veered dangerously close to Bryony's face.

"I'm going to get help," she informed him, gingerly stepping away from the chair. The man didn't seem to notice, instead sucking agitated air in through his teeth as his foot slipped and his knee connected with the wall.

This time when Bryony reached the office, the old woman was there, a black shawl wrapped around her shoulders despite the heat.

Bryony explained about the key, using mime to get her point across when her words were met with a blank stare.

"Ah," the old woman said at last. "In. Twist. Shake."

"In, twist, shake," repeated Bryony, and was rewarded with a crooked smile.

"Nai."

Bryony said the words again under her breath as she ventured back to the apartment, ignoring the increasingly ludicrous figure of the flailing man and moving confidently towards the door.

"In," she said, inserting the key.   ➥

"Twist," she whispered, turning it forcefully to the right.

"Shake," she finished, vibrating it.

Bryony closed her eyes, then gasped with joy as she pushed the door open.

At that exact same moment, the man finally managed to squeeze himself in through the window and slithered down the adjoining wall, landing on the bathroom tiles with a soft thud.

"Are you OK?" Bryony rushed in.

The man staggered upright and rubbed at the scrape on his knee.

"No," he said, and for a moment she thought he was going to start telling her off. Leon would have been apoplectic by this stage, and just the thought of him gave Bryony the strength she needed.

She folded her arms, daring the man to complain, and the two of them glared at each other for a second. Then, quite incredibly, he started to laugh.

"I'm a malaka," he told her happily, and Bryony laughed too, agreeing even though she had no idea what he was actually on about.

The man seemed to find this even funnier and slapped his thighs with pleasure as he laughed.

"You are funny," he informed her, and Bryony blushed. He was gorgeous, after all.

"We have a drink?" he said, stepping forwards and ushering her back towards the open door. "I take care of you."

He was so confident, so sure that she would go along with him willingly, and Bryony almost allowed herself to be persuaded. Ella would be so proud – this had been her plan all along.

But then Bryony thought about Leon, about how she had let him run her life, and how good it had felt just a few minutes ago to take that control back for herself.

"Sorry," she said, stopping as the man turned to look at her, his earlier frown returning and wrinkling his forehead. "But I'm actually very happy by myself." 🔘

JANE CORRY

Change For The Better

Sometimes it seems that Fate is against you – but it turns out she just has different plans...

If it hadn't been for the coffee shop, it might never have happened. But Emily had been lured by that deep, rich smell floating out as she walked past on her way to the interview.

"One cappuccino to take away please," she said to the girl at the counter.

There wasn't anyone in front of her so it shouldn't take long. But the girl was ages out there in the back. What was she doing? Emily glanced at her watch nervously. It wouldn't do to be late.

For two pins, she'd just go but she hadn't paid yet and Emily didn't like the idea of a small shop like this losing out.

"I'm so sorry," said the girl finally returning with her drink. She had a slight Italian accent. "There are problems with the machine and..."

"It doesn't matter." Emily didn't normally speak so brusquely but she was up against the clock! Thrusting a ten pound note into the girl's hand, she grabbed her change and ran out into the street.

Emily didn't like rushing. She prided herself on being nice and calm and organised, unlike her mother who had always been late for ➤

everything. Emily could still remember the shame of being the last one left at school, waiting to be collected…

"Whoops!" In her hurry, she'd collided with the bus stop. Now she'd gone and stained her skirt with the coffee! What sort of impression was that going to make at the interview? Still, at least the bus was here so with any luck she would still be on time.

"Haven't you got anything smaller, love?" asked the driver as she gave him a ten pound note.

"I should have," said Emily, opening her purse again. Oh, no! The Italian girl in the coffee shop must have mistakenly given her a fifty pound note instead of a five pound note, along with the two pounds fifty change!

The fifty pound note felt as if it was burning a hole in her hand

Emily was always careful to check her receipts. On the rare occasions when she'd been given too much – like now – Emily always went back and took pleasure in being thanked for her honesty.

But the bus was moving now and she had to stay on or she'd miss the interview.

Never mind, Emily tried to reassure herself. She'd return to the coffee shop later and put matters straight.

Taking a seat, Emily went through the papers in her bag to prepare for the interview. It was no good. She couldn't concentrate. The overpayment of fifty pounds was a lot for a small coffee shop. But it was also the principle that mattered – as she knew all too well.

How much longer is this going to take?" demanded the young man who was texting on his mobile.

"I am so sorry," replied Giulia with one of her best smiles. "The machine, she is slow this morning, but I will be as speedy as I can."

"Well I'm not waiting any longer."

"But please, you have ordered…"

Too late. The angry young man had gone. He wasn't the first. There had already been several abandoned coffees that morning because the customers couldn't wait. Hadn't she told her boss they needed a new machine? But it was she, Giulia, who had to take the brunt of it – as the dictionary said.

This was her favourite book along with her How To Learn English guide. Every night, before she went to sleep in her narrow bed, no matter how exhausted she was after her day, Giulia worked her way through, one letter a time.

At the moment, she was on the letter H. It was not an easy letter to say in this beautiful English language. She practised out loud now. "Huh! Huh for 'Hello'."

"What are you doing, harrumphing like that?" demanded a voice behind her. "And where have all the customers gone? There was a queue of them."

Giulia took a deep breath before turning round to face her boss.

"They would not wait. I tell you before, Mr Evans. The machine, she is old. She needs fixing."

"And I told you not to interfere. I pay you to serve, not complain." He opened the till. "How many coffees have you sold today?"

"Just one," she said, thinking of the tall woman with the beautiful auburn hair who had come in just after the shop had opened.

"Then perhaps you can explain why the fifty pound note in the float is missing?"

Giulia went hot and cold. It was so difficult to understand the difference between notes in this strange currency.

"I do not know."

"That's not good enough!" His short stubby finger jabbed at the till. "It's not the first time, is it? I might accept one honest mistake but this shows you are a thief! It's hardly worth me running this place. You can leave immediately."

"What about my wages?"

"It can pay for your errors. Now go. And take that How To Learn English book with you.'

Giulia's eyes filled with tears. She had to pay the rent on her tiny ➡

one bedroom flat. But most important, she needed to send money to Nonna back in Italy.

Now what was she going to do?

Emily got to the interview just in time. But she found it hard to concentrate on the questions and answers. That fifty pound note kept coming into her mind. It was silly really. But then, anyone who knew where she'd really come from, would understand.

"We'll be in touch."

Four simple words at the end of the interview which could mean the beginning or the end of so many hopes! Life, thought Emily, could be tough sometimes.

Thank goodness for David!

As if on cue, a text came up on her phone: *Everything all right?*

Tell you tonight, she texted back. Then she added, *Might be a bit late.*

But when Emily got to the coffee shop, the fifty pound note ready in her hand, there was a sign on the door: CLOSED UNTIL FURTHER NOTICE.

Oh no! Now she'd never be able to repay the money!

Emily felt terrible as she walked on round the corner. The note felt as if it was burning a hole in her hand.

"Got anything to spare, Miss?"

Normally Emily walked past people who begged. She didn't approve of giving them money in case they spent it on drugs or drink. But the fifty pound note that wasn't hers might as well go to a good cause.

"Please buy food with it," she said.

"I will, Miss. Don't you worry."

But she couldn't help fretting. When it came to money, Emily needed to know she was beyond reproach. And right now, she didn't feel she was.

Do not worry, my little one," soothed Nonna when Giulia used her precious phone card to ring home and explain what happened. "Something will come. I feel it in my bones. The important thing is that you are innocent. You did not take the money, no matter what your boss says. You are not like that."

But Giulia wondered how anyone knew what someone was really like.

"Evening, ducks," said the homeless man as Giulia went back to her flat.

"I'm so sorry I don't have anything for you today," she said.

"Don't you worry." He pointed to an empty chips and burger packet and rubbed his tummy, grinning. "I got lucky today – and there's enough for the rest of the week if I'm careful."

At least some kind person had helped him. But now she would be in trouble if she didn't find a job to pay the rent.

> *Emily would never forget when the police knocked on their door*

Then her eye fell on the free newspaper lying beside the homeless man. It was open at the Jobs column.

Quickly, Giulia picked it up.

Wanted, said an ad. *Bilingual assistant. Must be fluent in Italian and French.*

There was still time for her to apply. It was, as Nonna might have said, a sign.

G ood luck," said David kissing Emily goodbye the following morning as she made a sandwich for lunch. Emily smiled. Ever since their eyes had met at Business School, they'd known they were right for each other. But most important of all, David was an honest man.

He was also very understanding when she told him about her father being sent to prison when she was a child.

"I'll never forget the police knocking on our door because he'd defrauded his boss," she told him. "My mother had to do all kinds of jobs to keep us going, so she was often late picking me up from school. It made me stand out." ➤

Looking back, Emily realised she'd been too hard on her mother. Still, that was why she made sure Mum was comfortable now. It's why this job was so important to her.

Her route took her past the homeless man, still there on the corner.

"I thought you might like this," she said, handing him her sandwich.

"Thanks." He grinned toothily. "But I did what you said and bought food. So I'll give this sarnie to one of my mates."

"That's wonderful!" Emily walked on, her heart warm. It just went to show that you shouldn't judge others.

G iulia took one look at the big glass building and nearly ran away. This place was so smart!

"You can be anyone you want," Nonna always said. So, taking a deep breath, Giulia smoothed down her only skirt which she'd bought from the charity shop, and went in.

"I'm here for the bilingual assistant interview," she told the girl on the desk. "I phoned yesterday…"

The girl beamed, making Giulia instantly feel more relaxed.

"You're early. The boss will like that. Do go through."

Giulia was ushered into a bright airy room. The woman on the other side of the desk looked vaguely familiar.

"It's you," she said to Giulia. "The girl from the coffee shop."

Giulia's brain suddenly "clicked" as her English dictionary put it.

"I think I give you fifty-pound note instead of five."

Her interviewer flushed.

"I did come back at the end of the day but the shop was closed until further notice."

Giulia frowned. "Maybe because it loses my boss money. He sack me because of the mistake."

"I cost you your job? I'm so sorry!"

Giulia shrugged. "He also dislike my suggestion that he get a new machine to increase business."

"But that shows initiative," Emily exclaimed. Could she finally have found the right person to handle her new international client?

She didn't need anyone with numerate skills but the language was important – and so was honesty, as well as punctuality.

"Please sit down," Emily said.

"Thank you, Mrs Hall."

"Please. Call me Emily."

"I have a question before we start… what about the fifty pounds…?"

"I gave it to a good cause."

"Ah, that is good. My dictionary says that what goes round, comes round."

Emily put her coat on and kissed David goodbye. "Sure you don't want me to come too?" he asked.

"Thanks but this is something I need to do on my own."

It was true. This meeting wouldn't be easy but she had to be strong.

"I've put it behind me," her mother had said enough times over the years. "Can't you? Dad knows he did wrong but he's learned his lesson."

As Emily reached the small flat where her parents now lived, she couldn't help thinking that honesty was all very well – but as her bright new assistant had taught her, so too was forgiveness…

ABBIE GREAVES

The Snowglobe

Would her globe-trotting boyfriend ever fully become a part of Eloise's world? Or should she shake things up?

The thing is, we're a wholesaler which means we only do bulk orders. I'm afraid I can't sell you single pencils..."

Eloise checked the dashboard on her phone. Five minutes and forty-three seconds. She didn't know it could take anyone that long to cotton on to concept of a twelve-unit minimum order.

"But I have been recommended to Only Office Supplies by a friend and he said..."

Here we go, Eloise thought, *another five minutes of my Wednesday morning wasted. Although the gentleman on the other end of the line does sound a bit doddery, bless him.* She could sit back, zone out and consider this a nap. One with her eyes wide open.

Eloise had just the thing for her fidgeting hands. Just the things, rather. Beneath her computer screen sat twenty snow globes, each from a different city in the world. They were gifts from Mark over the course of the four years that they had been together.

All the trips had been solo. For business, Eloise reminded herself, before the spark of resentment in her belly caught light. It wasn't his fault that his sales role was significantly more glamorous than hers.

It was work they had bonded over when they had first met in the ⬛m – a horrible cliché, Eloise could appreciate. But then Mark had ⬛n so persuasive, catching her outside the changing rooms with shower-fresh hair, asking if she was free for dinner there and then. He had shown himself to be funny, sharp and charming. So very charming.

And just like that, he had tilted her world on its head. Love always left Eloise feeling impossibly giddy.

She picked up the first of the globes and shook it. She repeated the process with two, three, four more, wanting to see how many she could make snow at once.

"Well – I shall be taking my custom elsewhere," the caller huffed.

Eloise opened her mouth to reply, but the line had already gone dead.

She urgently needed a new job. Only Office Supplies had started off as a stopgap after university but at some point, it had become a permanent contract that Eloise couldn't shake. Sometimes, she hoped Mark might suggest new job opportunities for her – after all, he had so many connections – but he never took the hint.

It wasn't just those hints Mark didn't pick up on. Eloise was desperate to move in together – to his place or to hers, it didn't matter. What mattered was that they started to build a proper future together. She wanted a family. Mark said he did too, "when the time was right".

But when was that? Mark would be forty next month. Eloise was thirty-four.

She traced her finger around the base of her favourite snow globe, the one with a row of children painted onto the porcelain, trembling with longing.

They were due to have dinner at the weekend, when Mark was back from Boston. Eloise had told herself she would bring up the subject of kids then. But how would he respond to that conversation? Mark had been so odd of late, alternately aloof and snappy.

The phone burbled. Eloise prayed Pencil-man wasn't back for round two. But before she could get her greeting in, the caller started talking. It was a voice she knew almost better than her own.

"Just a quick one, Amanda. I'll be back tonight..."

Amanda? Had Mark got a new secretary? Eloise opened her mouth but her gut warned her to keep shtum. ➙

"I've booked a room at the Marriott near the station. Meet me there at seven? I've got a table reserved and a little something to show how I've missed you."

Eloise thought she was about to be sick in her mug. Everything was falling into place – the irritability, the nights when he didn't respond to her calls, the lack of commitment to a future with her…

"Mandy – are you there?"

"Wrong number," Eloise replied.

"Oh God…"

Eloise didn't wait to hear his botched apology. She grabbed the bin and with the other hand, knocked the snow globes into it. For a few seconds, she absorbed the full snowstorm of pain, anger and humiliation. Then came a sunbeam of realisation.

Eloise opened her mouth, but her gut warned her to keep shtum and listen

It wasn't just Mark who hadn't been himself, was it? It was Eloise too. She barely recognised the woman who meekly accepted the fluctuations in his mood.

The hope that he might change had been so bright that it almost blinded her. Almost. Mark's misdial could turn out to be a blessing in disguise.

Eloise knew the blizzard of upset would pass and when it did, she would return to her old self again. A little wiser.

She bent down and retrieved a fragment of snow globe from her feet – the one with the porcelain children.

Only Eloise could build the life she wanted. Now, at least, there was no one to hold her back. ⓜ